THE BIG GROUSE

THE BIG GROUSE

DOUGLAS CLARK

PERENNIAL LIBRARY

Harper & Row, Publishers, New York
Cambridge, Philadelphia, San Francisco, Washington
London, Mexico City, São Paulo, Singapore, Sydney

First PERENNIAL LIBRARY edition published 1988.

Library of Congress Cataloging-in-Publication Data

Clark, Douglas.
  The big grouse.

  I. Title.
[PR6053.L294B5   1988b]   823′.914   87-46129
ISBN 0-06-080918-3 (pbk.)

---

88 89 90 91 92 OPM 10 9 8 7 6 5 4 3 2 1

THE BIG GROUSE

1

Detective Chief Superintendent George Masters sat at his desk and drew the top package in the tray towards him. He noticed with some pleasure that the pile was appreciably smaller than it had been for several days, the result of the clerical thrash which was inevitably his lot when there was something of a break in major cases involving him personally or his whole team of DS Reed, DS Berger and former DCI Bill Green, now theoretically an SSCO at the yard.

The file he had selected caused him mixed emotions. It was Reed's personal record, sent to him sealed in a large outer envelope and marked "Confidential— Addressee Only." He knew what to expect as he opened the cover. Reed had passed his promotion board. Masters was more than pleased about that. Reed was a competent man and had proved himself on many an occasion. His promotion was, if anything, long overdue, and but for the reluctance of the Yard hierarchy to break up successful teams, Reed would have become a Divisional DI at least a year earlier.

Masters mused on the fact that success should hamper a man's career. The cream didn't always rise to the top. Sometimes it was the scum that had that privilege. Now, however, Reed would be in more of a position to shape his future for himself. Masters was delighted at the thought. He was, at the same time, saddened by the idea of losing Reed who, as a colleague of some years' standing, had also become a friend. A friend not only of Masters, Green and Berger, but of Masters' wife, Wanda,

1

and Green's wife, Doris. Since Masters' marriage and the birth of his son, the team he headed had become welded into an homogeneous whole—both on and off parade. When this happened, there grew up a rare understanding which enhanced the proficiency of the squad on those cases where all members were required to work together.

He took up his pen. He was asked to note the fact of Reed's promotion and to add a recommendation as to the type of job best suited to Reed's abilities—with reasons. A normal DI in Central London or further out, in the suburbs which came within the Metropolitan area? Any particular Squad? Narcotics, Flying, Special, Bomb? Masters thought it all through carefully. He had written a report on Reed for consideration by the Promotions Board before the interview. That had been more of a general recommendation. Now he had to be more specific. It was a serious matter. In the right job, Reed would flourish. In the wrong one. . . .

He had just finished and had resealed the envelope when there was a rap on the door and Bill Green poked his head in.

"Busy, George?"

"Good morning, Bill. Yes, I'm busy. You're the lucky one. In your present situation I don't suppose you get as much paper work as you used to."

"You're joking," said Green, coming into the office and, uninvited, taking a visitor's chair. "There's enough bumph floating round this wigwam to make a waste-paper merchant a millionaire within a month. Memos, dockets, notices . . . I get them all, and I read 'em. Just to keep abreast, you know."

"And?"

"It still leaves me time to pick up rumours."

"What this time?"

"Young Reed."

"What about him?"

"He's already on the casualty list. Promoted as from today. That means we've lost him, George, unless they're

2

thinking of giving you a DI again, in place of me, and booting me out."

Masters realized suddenly that underneath his apparent nonchalance, Green was worried. Probably had been worried for some time over the possible changes that could be made when Reed secured his promotion. Green, standing-in, on a temporary basis, would naturally have qualms lest the somewhat nebulous arrangement that kept him on after normal retirement should now be ended. Masters hastened to reassure him.

"I've just been asked to write a recommendation as to Reed's future employment. I've said it is time he was given the chance to get out and about on his own, free from the overprotective influence you and I must have on him. He's ready to test his wings."

Green grunted—presumably with satisfaction and in agreement with what Masters had said.

"Replacement?" he asked.

"No firm decision yet," replied Masters. "I have mentioned it upstairs, but I was told that no selection has so far been made, although there are, apparently, a number of volunteers."

"You mean somebody has made a request to join us?"

"Strange as it may seem, yes. Several of them. But I expect I shall be given a shortlist from which to choose."

"Shall you take Berger as your personal sidekick in place of Reed?"

"I think not, Bill. Berger will obviously be the senior of the two, but you and he have always worked together. I can see little point in causing more disruption than necessary."

"Thanks. Berger knows me. A newcomer might not take so kindly to siding with a has-been like me."

"There's that, of course. But we're a team, Bill. Whoever we get will have to recognize the authority I accord you within it, irrespective of your official standing."

"Ta. I was hoping. . . ."

"What?"

"That you'd say something along those lines."

"Don't thank me, Bill. Apart from my own pleasure at having you along, the AC (Crime) asked me recently if I thought you'd be willing to continue. He wants you to."

"Anderson does?"

"Why not? The arrangement has paid dividends, hasn't it? His main aim and object is to register successes, irrespective of who chalks them up for him. As long as we keep bringing home the bacon he'll keep you on till you're tripping over your beard. And—apart from that—he has a certain regard for you, Bill."

"You mean he's grown used to having me around," grunted Green, obviously trying to hide the delight he was feeling at what Masters had said.

"Something like that," grinned Masters. "Our Edgar never shows much feeling, but he's bright enough to know on which side his bread is buttered."

Green took out his usual crumpled pack of cigarettes and lit one. It was obvious to Masters that his colleague, having satisfactorily clarified the point that had been worrying him, now intended to stay to chat. This was not usual because Green, though frequently garrulous when out of the office, was normally businesslike enough not to waste his own or others' working time. So Masters refrained from pointedly taking the next file from his in-tray and sat back, prepared to listen.

"Has young Reed said anything to you about getting married?" asked Green at last.

"Married?" Masters sat forward in his chair. "Nothing at all. This is the first I've heard of it. Who's the girl?"

"Muriel."

"Muriel who? Should I know her?"

"The little blonde WPC we took with us on the Chinemouth job two or three months ago."

Masters nodded his remembrance of the girl. "Muriel of Muriel and Irene."

"That's the one."

"He's kept it very quiet. I didn't even know they were friends or whatever couples call themselves in the prelude to marriage these days."

"There's been a bit of courting," said Green. "I've known about it, but I hadn't realized it had got quite as far as it appears to have done. Young Berger told me this morning that Reed was only waiting for his promotion to be announced officially before becoming engaged."

"I see. I think it's a good thing for an officer to be married by the time he becomes an inspector and you and I can't find much fault with the wedded state, can we, Bill?"

"None at all, I reckon. Depends on the personalities, of course."

"Are you hinting that, in your opinion, the girl is not the right one for Reed?"

"Not at all. I thought she was a nice little totty. They both were. Nice, competent, level headed and not bad to look at, either. What more could any bloke ask?"

Masters shrugged.

Green said: "I just thought I'd tell you the buzz. Not that it's any of our business now, but Wanda and Doris will want to know."

"Not before it's official. Then, I think we could have a little party, for old times' sake. We could combine it with a congratulatory drink for Reed on his promotion."

"At your place?"

"I think so, don't you? Our two girls will want to join in and I certainly don't want to drag them into some drunken orgy at a pub."

Green got to his feet. "Fair enough. It's mighty nice of you and Wanda. . . ."

"Rubbish, Bill. Doris will do some of the work, won't she?"

"Try and keep her away from it," grinned Green.

"Good. Let me know when there's anything decided, please, Bill."

Green left the office.

Masters had read another file and added a few brief notes before the next interruption came.

Anderson, AC (Crime), on the internal phone.

"Two points to discuss, George. Are you free to come up for a chat?"

It didn't sound as though Anderson was proposing to send him off on some immediate investigation, so Masters did not bother to give the members of his team the usual prepare-to-move warning. He went up to the floor above the one on which his own office was situated and asked Anderson's secretary to tell the AC of his arrival.

"Come in, George." Edgar Anderson, sitting at his desk, peered over the spectacles he had recently started to wear for close work. "Sit down."

Masters took the chair opposite the AC.

"How's Wanda keeping? And the boy?"

"They are both fine, thank you. Mrs Anderson is enjoying this good weather, I hope?"

Anderson removed his spectacles and sat back. "Thoroughly enjoying it, George, thank you, except. . . ."

Masters waited a moment or two.

"Is there something wrong, sir? I know when you last dined with us Mrs Anderson told Wanda she'd got a bit of back trouble which her doctor was unable to diagnose exactly."

Anderson waved one hand, gently, as if to dismiss his wife's ailment as trivial. "It cleared itself up. Muscle strain or some such from hanging the curtains or trying to shift furniture to hoover under it."

"I see. But there's some cloud on the horizon?"

"Yes. Not her immediate concern, but in her family." Masters waited again, wondering of what interest this private worry of Mrs Anderson's might be to him. "Distant family," amended Anderson. "Cousin's daughter's husband—that sort of thing."

Anderson was being diffident for some reason. Masters decided he had better ask the obvious question in order to speed matters up.

"What's happened to him?"

"Disappeared. Wife, work colleagues, bank . . . nobody's heard of him for some months now."

"Have the police in the area been asked to help?"

"What area?"

"Where he lives and works."

"Oh, I see. Sorry to sound vague, George, but he's a rep, this chap, so he wasn't always at home during the working week. So nobody is quite sure where he disappeared from, if you get my meaning."

Masters nodded. "And the local police have taken a polite but unenthusiastic interest, as one might expect? I mean, married men disappear in their scores every week. Usually to run away from their own wives or to run to somebody else's. All legal. The police can't look for them and haul them back, not unless there's a suggestion of crime concerning the disappearance."

Anderson nodded. "That's what I've told my missus repeatedly, but she thinks we ought to be able to do something."

"By we, does she mean the police in general, sir, or those of us under your particular command?"

Anderson shrugged. "The latter. She keeps on about how we're supposed to have scores of clever detectives here at the Yard, so why can't we show how clever we are by producing this missing joker. Of course her cousin's pestering her about it, but. . . ."

"But you can't get the explanation through to her. Is that it, sir?"

"I suppose so. I don't think Beryl is being particularly obtuse. If this business affected anybody else—somebody not in her family or of whom she was not particularly fond—she would see and appreciate our point of view with no bother at all. But she and this cousin of hers grew up together. Actually, they lived next door to each other in adjoining semis. Their respective parents lived in each other's pockets, with all the in-laws on both sides living within a mile. Just like it always was in those days before families got into the modern habit of breaking up and moving out of their native areas to find work."

"Self-supporting—or supportive—family groups," murmured Masters.

"Just so. It was like that for most people—before your

7

time, of course, but I'm not sure it wasn't a better state of affairs, particularly for the older members of each clan. However. . . ."

"Are you asking me for my thoughts on the business of the missing man, sir, or are you suggesting that I should actively try to find him?"

"What I want from you, George, is something to satisfy Beryl. By that, I mean I'd like you to dictate a memo addressed to me suggesting all the usual steps anybody can take to trace a man. Inform the Salvation Army, hire a private detective . . . you know the sort of thing. Then I can hand it to Beryl and tell her I've consulted the one and only George Masters about her problem and this is his answer or considered opinion or whatever, and hope she'll at last be satisfied. She'll take your word for it better than she will mine."

Masters smiled his understanding. "I'll make it good and comprehensive," he promised. "To show we've really taken the trouble to help."

"Excellent. Sorry to put you to so much trouble, George, but you must know how it is when one's wife can't or won't understand that private concerns and official business can't always be merged."

Masters nodded in reply. Not that Wanda had ever— so far, at any rate—caused him the same dilemma, but her curiosity had, at times, led her to enquire a little too closely into confidential police affairs and he had been obliged on occasions to dissemble slightly to head her off. Not that he objected to such curiosity. He welcomed his wife's enthusiastic interest in his work. He thought it good for both of them, but he tried never to lose sight of the fact that some of his knowledge and activities had to be kept from her, if only in the interests of criminals.

Anderson continued to talk. "Can you let me have the memo today, George? The sooner I can show it to Beryl, the better."

Masters recalled the diminishing pile of paperwork on his desk and promised he would get his team to work and let the AC have the memo during the course of the afternoon.

"Excellent. And don't forget to sign the damn thing yourself, George. Your name at the bottom will go a long way towards satisfying Beryl that we've done what we could. Now. . . ." Anderson reached for a file in his tray. "You've heard that Reed has been promoted? I haven't sent you an official notice about a replacement because I wanted to talk to you about it first." Anderson looked up. "Have you anybody specific in mind?"

"A detective sergeant? No, sir. I could, of course, sound out Bill Green and DS Berger on the subject. They're more likely to know of suitable candidates than I am, simply because they have more to do with. . . ."

"Don't bother them about it," interrupted Anderson. "You'd have to make the final choice in any case and I'd rather you didn't try to recruit from somebody else's firm. What I mean is, George, that I don't want the impression to get about that you can have the pick of anybody you want and that an assignment to your team is a form of step-up inside the rank of DS. That would be bad and, in any case, would tend to weaken the firm you recruited from—presuming you chose the ablest of the DSs on offer."

"I get the drift, sir."

"No." Anderson shook his head. "No, an established team such as yours is an ideal training ground for the inexperienced, George. With Bill Green and Sergeant Berger alongside you, you can afford to bring somebody on from scratch and not notice the early shortcomings."

"We took on Berger when he was a Detective Constable," agreed Masters. "But Bill Green had had an eye on him for some time before we needed him."

"He'd vetted him?"

"He'd certainly used him on several small jobs before the vacancy arose."

Anderson sat quiet for a moment. "Now, George, I don't want you to take this the wrong way, but I'm not going to give you any choice in this matter."

Masters grinned and raised his eyebrows.

"No?"

"I am making the appointment for you."

Masters didn't reply. This wasn't Anderson speaking. Something was afoot. Some pressure had been brought to bear on the AC to cause him to adopt this attitude. It was out of character. Normally he would have told Masters to go ahead and make his own choice, rubber-stamping the suggestion as soon as it had been made. So what was going on? Anybody who could pressurize Anderson would need to be pretty high up in the hierarchy. Probably only the Commissioner would have the necessary clout. For what? Favouritism? Nepotism? Masters didn't like the idea of either: had almost decided on instant refusal or rebellion, when Anderson went on half-ashamedly.

"Policy, George."

So Anderson's hand had been forced, but apparently not on behalf of any one candidate.

Masters waited.

"Women," said Anderson. "We're being accused of not giving the distaff side equal opportunities for advancement within the force. I agreed with that when it was put to me and said that we in Crime would do all we possibly could to make sure our girls got a fair crack of the promotion whip."

Masters nodded. "I'm in agreement with that, too, sir. But. . . ."

"But what, George?"

"But I think there are two provisos. One, that the woman in question should be as professional as her male rivals for the job, and not secure the appointment for the sake of satisfying feminist clamour. Two, that she should be able to take care of herself in the rough and tumble of field work."

Anderson scratched the bridge of his nose with one finger before replying. "There is talk of percentages

10

among appointees," he murmured apologetically. "Thirty per cent women to seventy per cent men."

"Irrespective of ability, suitability and everything else, sir?"

"So it seems, George."

"Under which pressure you propose to replace Reed with a woman detective sergeant?"

Anderson grimaced. "I wouldn't have thought you would have objected to a woman in your team, George."

"I don't. But I do object to having somebody foisted on me in the name of sexual equality irrespective of suitability for the job. If the woman you send me measures up to the job, well and good. If not. . . ." He shrugged and left the sentence unfinished.

"And I would support you in that," said Anderson, "were it not for one thing."

"What's that, sir?"

"Bill Green's position. I had to fight off a demand that you should take a woman DI in his place. I was on sticky ground there. I only managed to keep him on by promising you'd take a woman sergeant as Reed's replacement."

"I see," said Masters quietly. "Virtual blackmail."

"Total blackmail," growled Anderson. "They sent me a list of three to choose from, but I did what I could as a protest. I refused them all."

Masters grinned. "Did that make you feel better about it, sir?"

"Much."

"What has happened?"

"By way of riposte, you mean? Nothing. I've appointed a woman DS who asked to join you. One you know and who knows you."

Masters looked astounded. "But I don't know any women DSs, sir."

"You know this one. She's just been promoted. Irene Tippen. You took her with you last summer down to Chinemouth. She obviously liked working with you then,

11

because she asked to join you some weeks ago."

Masters laughed. "Did she indeed? Of course I remember her. The dark-haired one who posed as Bill Green's daughter. She's obviously a bit of an opportunist."

"How d'you mean?"

"DS Reed is about to announce his engagement to her friend, WPC Clegg. . . ."

"The other one who went with you?"

"The same. Tippen must have learned weeks ago that Reed would be leaving me and, knowing her own promotion to sergeant was also due, put in a bid for his job."

"Initiative," grunted Anderson. "Anyhow, I've decided she'll come to you."

"Right, sir. Does she know yet?"

"She'll be told this morning. She'll report to your office before lunch."

Masters got to his feet.

"And don't forget that other business, George."

"You'll have the memo quite soon, sir."

Irene Tippen knocked on Masters' door soon after half past eleven. She waited for the summons to enter, smoothing down the civilian skirt which, as a member of CID, she was entitled to wear. She knew she was excited but hoped it wasn't nervousness at the prospect of again working with Masters and his team.

"Come in."

"I got a message to come and see you, sir."

Masters got to his feet. "Nice to see you again . . . er . . . Sergeant Tippen. Congratulations on the promotion."

"Thank you, sir."

"Sit down." As she took the chair, he said, "Did the message telling you to report to me also inform you that you will be joining my team?"

"Yes, sir."

"You asked to come to us?"

"Yes, sir."

"Why?"

The girl paused a moment. "I really do know why, sir,

but it would take an awful lot of explaining. After having worked with you I knew that it wasn't just CID work I wanted, but your particular blend of it. The way you and the others work. . . ." She paused, reddening under his gaze. "I felt it was right for me," she added quietly after the silence.

"I can think of no better reason," said Masters, helping her out. "Do you know your stuff?"

"Yes, sir." Confident.

"Photographs? Dabs? Driving?"

"All of those, sir."

"Good passes?"

"Yes, sir."

"Initiative test?"

She looked down.

"Pass not so good, eh?"

"No, sir. I just got through."

"What let you down? Practical or Viva?"

"Viva, sir. It was . . . complicated."

"What was, the question?"

"Yes, sir. I got flummoxed."

Masters laughed aloud. "Names, dates, timings?"

"And the legal side, sir. They told me I had encountered a solicitor under suspicious circumstances. One who knew all the answers."

"What you could and could not legally do without arresting him?"

She nodded.

"Don't worry. Experience will teach you that."

"I hope so, sir. I made a mess of it."

"I suspect you were expected to. But the board couldn't have been all that displeased with you. Now, what job have you got on at the moment?"

"None, sir. I was told to hand over before. . . ."

"Good. Now, Sergeant, you will work directly with me."

She was surprised. "But what about Sergeant Berger?"

"He'll continue to work with DCI Green. So, you've got to take over the car, the bags and other equipment. Berger will help you with that. And there's one other job

13

I want you to do for me." Masters proceeded to tell her the story about Mrs Anderson's cousin's daughter's husband. "Your job is to write a memo as to what steps the members of Mrs Anderson's family should take to try to trace the missing man." He gave her an outline of what he thought those steps should be. "Get that written up for me in a form acceptable for the AC's wife. Make it fairly full, so that it looks as though we had taken some trouble over it. Let me have it by three o'clock."

"Right sir. May I ask a question?"

"Of course."

"Is this simply a test you are setting me, or is it a true case?"

"It's an actual disappearance and, yes, I want to see how well you can handle it. How many suggestions you can make, how many lines of exploration you think there may be . . . but you don't need me to tell you any more, otherwise I might as well do it myself."

She got to her feet.

"Just one more question," said Masters. "What would you like us to call you? Sergeant Tippen or Irene or what?"

She replied with a straight face. "I'm known as Tip, mostly, sir. Very few people call me Irene."

"Very nice, too. I shall call you Tip. I can't vouch for what DCI Green will christen you."

"In the past it has varied, sir. From love to petal."

Masters grinned. "Very much as I would expect. OK, Tip, off you go and get on with things."

"Thank you sir."

It was just a few minutes to three that same afternoon when the outside phone on Masters' desk rang. He had emptied his in-tray and was awaiting Tip's arrival with the memo he had instructed her to write. He put down on his blotter the pipe he was packing with Warlock Flake.

"DCS Masters."

"Would you hold for a moment, sir. I have Mrs Anderson for you."

"*Mrs* Anderson? The wife of the AC (Crime)?"

"Yes, sir."

"Are you sure she wants to speak to me?"

"Yes, sir. Perfectly sure."

Masters groaned inwardly. He guessed Edgar Anderson had told Beryl that he, Masters, had been asked to look at the problem of the missing relative, and that she was now ringing up for a progress report.

"Put Mrs Anderson through please."

"George?"

"Beryl."

"George, I'm ringing to tell you that your new young lady sergeant, Miss Tippen, will be a few minutes late for your three o'clock meeting. She seemed so very worried about not being on time on her very first day with you that I said I would ring you and put it right."

"What's been happening, Beryl?"

"Oh, I held her up. She wanted to get away at half past two, but I kept her. It's entirely my fault, so don't be too hard on her, George."

"Get away from where at half past two?"

"From here, of course."

"Your house, Beryl?"

"Yes. So good of you to put such a nice young lady on to the case, George. I knew when Edgar said he would ask you about things that there would soon be some action."

"Yes, Beryl. But I didn't want DS Tippen calling at your house and worrying you at this stage."

"Oh, I asked her to come, George. I thought it would be so much better than just a phone call, and of course, it was. Now you are going to start an enquiry. . . ?"

"Beryl."

". . . I feel sure everything will be all right."

"Beryl."

"Yes, George?"

"I don't know what DS Tippen has said to you, but as yet we have no real grounds for starting an enquiry, and even were there to be a reason, there is no certainty that I should deal with it. I handle murder cases mostly, not missing persons."

"Oh, I see you haven't heard the latest turn of events. But of course you haven't. That clever girl of yours hasn't seen you, has she, since you first told her to start work?"

"No, she hasn't," said Masters heavily.

"Oh, well, she'll be at the Yard any minute now and she'll tell you all about it. I shall be able to say 'Snubs to you, Edgar Anderson' when he gets home tonight. He's been trying to put me off for months about this, but I knew that as soon as I insisted he should speak to you about it. . . ."

"I've been away from the Yard for two or three months, Beryl, and for some months before that I was working on a very important job totally unconnected with the AC. . . ."

"Yes, yes, I know, George. And you've been wounded, too, that's why I didn't press Edgar about my problem until I knew you were really back on duty. I'll ring off now, George, because that girlie of yours will be with you any moment now. 'Bye, George. Love to Wanda."

Masters put the phone down and picked up his pipe. What had the girl got up to, he wondered. If it turned out to be something upsetting for Edgar Anderson, the AC had only himself to blame. He had appointed Irene Tippen to the firm, so he would have to bear the consequences of what appeared to be a bad case of over enthusiasm on the part of the girl.

As he put a match to the tobacco he began to wonder what on earth Tip could have said to cause Beryl Anderson to think that there was now a case to investigate.

Three or four minutes later, DS Tippen herself appeared.

"Sorry I'm late, sir."

"Mrs Anderson rang to say she had held you up."

"She did talk rather a lot, sir, but I didn't feel I could

16

be rude to the AC's wife and rush away while she was in midstream."

"Quite. The point is not what she said to you, but what you said to her." Masters tipped out his pipe and left it in the ashtray. "Sit down and tell me what's been going on."

"Well, sir, you said I had to write a complete memo and make a good job of it."

Masters nodded.

"So I took advice, sir."

"Fair enough. Who from?"

"Mr Green and Missing Persons. They both told me that there were certain steps people could take for themselves as you did. One of the ones you didn't mention was for the family to find out from his firm his projected route for the week in which he disappeared and to try the hotels he might have stayed at. Oh, and all sorts of things like that. Ask his customers on that particular route whether he called that week and so on."

Masters murmured his appreciation of the points mentioned.

"Everybody I spoke to emphasized that any adult can do a disappearing act if he or she wants to, that it is not a criminal act, and that the police cannot interfere unless there is a crime involved."

"Quite right."

"I'd got it all together, sir, but I thought I ought to have the man's name and the date of his disappearance. To make the memo look . . . well, a proper job, sir. You hadn't given me this information, and I couldn't go on referring to him as Mrs Anderson's cousin's daughter's husband. So I came to ask you, but you weren't here. And I didn't think I ought to bother the AC (Crime). . . ."

Masters grinned. "It would be a bit intimidating for a sprog sergeant to beard the AC in his office."

"Yes, sir. So I rang Mrs Anderson."

"Ah! A tactical error, Tip."

"I realize that now, sir. She asked me why I wanted the information and I told her I didn't really know but that it was to include in a memo for you."

"Go on."

"She said something about her husband having at last asked you to take the matter in hand and that now there would be some action."

"What was your reply to that?"

"I said I didn't think you would be able to do anything because no crime had been involved and she wasn't to build her hopes up. She asked me what I meant, so I told her that Mr Louis Packard—that's the distant relative by marriage who has disappeared—had committed no crime nor, as far as we knew, had anybody committed a crime against him. That meant that the police had no reason to interfere."

"What did she say?"

"Sir, I thought she was satisfied with what I had told her, but in less than half an hour she called me back. That was at twenty to two and. . . ."

"It seems to me, young lady, that you'd skipped lunch and worked right through."

"Well, yes, sir, but. . . ."

"I admire your dedication, but I admire more the ability to do a job on time *and* have lunch. Our sort of work often means working long hours for days on end. A member of the team that doesn't take necessary sustenance can wilt under the strain. Understood?"

"Yes, sir."

"Good. Carry on. Mrs Anderson rang you."

"She asked me to go round immediately as she had some important news. I didn't think I could refuse, sir."

"You couldn't. What was her news?"

"After I spoke to her she'd rung Louis Packard's wife and told her what I said. They'd then put their heads together and rung Packard's employers."

"And?"

"When they heard what Mrs Packard had to say they immediately agreed to accuse Louis Packard of crime."

"What sort of crime?"

"Chiefly the theft of a valuable company car, sir. They haven't seen it since, you see. And they added all manner

18

of things. Samples. Books of secret specifications, a portable display stand, free gifts. Even the document case he used was theirs. Oh, and a cash float. Each of their reps has a hundred pounds of company money at all times. As they use it they claim to make it up to the hundred again."

Masters sat silent for a moment.

"What did you say to Mrs Anderson?"

"I tried to argue her out of it, sir. Very cautiously, of course. I said the company would have been recompensed by insurance and they wouldn't be anxious to pursue the matter as far as involving the police, but she would have none of it. She kept smiling at me and saying what a good job I was doing by going into all the possibilities so thoroughly and by playing devil's advocate to make sure there really was a criminal element in the disappearance. In the end, sir. . . ."

"She wore you down?"

"Not quite, but I had to come away without having convinced her that it really wasn't a job for a murder team. She seemed so sure you would be given it as a case."

"I know Mrs Anderson," said Masters, as if to say he appreciated all the difficulties Tip had encountered. "Well, now, you seem to have stirred up a bit of trouble for the AC. Get it all typed up . . . you can type, I hope."

"I was a typist before I joined the force, sir."

"Good. So you'll be able to let me have the memo I originally asked for, just as I asked for it."

"Just that bit, sir?"

"And a separate note to cover Mrs Anderson's claim that a crime was involved. I'll take the matter from there."

"Thank you, sir. I'm sorry if. . . ."

"Don't be sorry, Tip. Our job is to be thorough. I would rather you hadn't rung Mrs Anderson. But the bit about our not being involved except in the case of crime would have appeared in the memo in any case, and Mrs Anderson would have seized on that this evening as soon as the AC showed it to her. So there's no milk spilt, and

I'll be able to forewarn the AC as to the line his wife will take when he gets home tonight. Then it's up to him."

Green joined Masters a few minutes after Irene Tippen had gone.

"She told me you'd signed her up," said Green.

"Not me. Anderson. Under pressure from the percentage people."

"Percentage? Oh, I know. Equal opportunities an' all that. But I'm still surprised that Anderson took her for your firm."

"You should take it as a great compliment to yourself that he did."

Green selected a cigarette carefully. "I could read that as meaning that I'll be present as a father figure to look after her, but I suspect there's a different explanation."

Masters grinned. "Somebody got the bright idea that a woman DI should take your place. Anderson refused to contemplate that."

"Is that the truth?"

"Absolutely. But having stood firm over you he had to compromise by accepting a women DS. Even then he dug his toes in and selected young Tip, who wasn't one of those recommended for selection."

"Good for Edgar."

"Tip had volunteered as soon as she was promoted."

"Good for her. I like the little lady. She and Muriel Clegg were worth their keep down in Chinemouth. I hope you're not too unhappy about her becoming a permanent fixture, George."

"I'm not." Masters laughed aloud. "She's only been with us a matter of hours, and she's already pulled a flanker on Anderson."

"How come?"

Master recounted the story of Tip's first job and how it seemed highly probable that Beryl Anderson would be able to force the AC's hand.

"I like it," said Green. "But what can Edgar do about it? Personally, I mean. It'll have to be put into the hands of whichever County force covers the ground where he disappeared. Did Edgar say where that was?"

Masters shook his head. "He doesn't know. He couldn't tell me. I'll ask him again when I take the memo upstairs and warn him that the ground has been cut from under his feet by those two ladies, Tip and Beryl."

Green grunted with laughter at the thought.

He changed his tune shortly after half past nine the next morning when Masters called him in.

"Have you got much on, Bill? You and Berger?"

"Several small bits and pieces. At least Berger has. I'm helping."

"What, specifically?"

"The break-in at the Pakistani late-night grocer's. The one where one of the young tearaways got cut so badly on broken glass."

"How's it going?"

"Fairly well, we think. We've located a doctor who was called in to a so-called domestic accident."

"So-called?"

Green nodded. "One of these night locums. Arrived at the house to find a youth gashed to glory and a window in the room broken and covered with blood. The doc called an ambulance and the man was carted off to be stitched up."

"Go on."

"Berger and I were doing a bit of sniffing round the hospitals and when we heard about this one we reckoned the domestic scene had been rigged so as not to arouse the doctor's suspicions. He had told the hospital it was an accident in the home. We reckon it was a wound received in the shop raid."

"How did you get on to it?"

"Fairly easily, really. The shopkeeper told us that the glass had actually cut through the fabric of the yobbo's shirt sleeve. Evidently he yelped like hell and rolled the sleeve up to see the damage. There was a snake tattoo on his forearm. The Pakistani managed to get such a good view because when the villain saw the damage the glass had done to his arm he virtually passed out, so his two mates had to carry him away. The bloody arm was dangling, showing the tattoo. The shopkeeper and his daughter both remembered it, so we were away. It seemed as though it could be a hospital job, so we carried on from there."

"So it's virtually finished?"

"Loose ends to be tied up. Blood to be matched—shop, house and villain—a three way cert. That sort of thing."

"Which Berger can manage alone, presumably?"

"As easy as kiss your old whatsisname. Why are you asking?"

Masters sat back. "I was called in to see Anderson as soon as he arrived this morning. It took me a minute or two to convince him that young Tip hadn't upset the applecart and that she'd only anticipated events by an hour or two."

"I hope you pointed out to him that if he hadn't asked for a stupid memo, signed by you, to convince his missus, nothing at all would have happened."

"I put it slightly more diplomatically than that."

"That 'ud please him, however you put it."

"Quite. However, the upshot is that we have now to be seen to make a token gesture to please Beryl."

"We? You mean you, don't you?"

"The firm. Only because we're already implicated."

"You're not going to. . . ."

"No, Bill. I'm going to give it to Tip, seeing she is already involved. But I want you to hold her hand. Look at it as a training exercise for her if you like, and steer her clear of any more excesses of enthusiasm which might land us in the soup."

Green grimaced. "As you know, I don't mind holding the hand of any bit of capurtle like young Tip, but I can't see there's a lot we can do."

"I hope there isn't. I don't want us wasting our time chasing stolen cars. Just try to get hold of something we can hand over to the people who are best able to deal with such things and that will be that. It will get Beryl Anderson off our backs."

"Will do." Green got to his feet. "The little lass will drive, will she?"

"She should have taken the car over from Reed by now. Oh, and please let Berger know that he's to carry on on his own."

That was the last Masters saw of Green during the working day, but at about seven o'clock in the evening the DCI and his wife, Doris, arrived at the door of the little house behind Westminster Hospital. They were frequent visitors and so their coming caused no surprise, though Wanda had to go through to the kitchen and—with Doris' help—hurriedly wash more lettuce and scrub more new potatoes for boiling.

"Slice plenty of tomatoes and cucumber," she said to Doris, "while I lay another two places at table. There's plenty of cold ham and we can eke out the strawberries with ice cream."

"We shouldn't have come unannounced," wailed Doris. "I told Bill, but he was insistent that he should see George. No fooling about, as he usually does."

"Workmanlike, was he?"

"Serious, certainly."

"Oh, well, they're nattering away now in the sitting-room. Whatever it is, they'll sort it out between them."

They were not sorting anything out. Green was merely reporting his fears.

"There's something wrong, George."

"Gut feeling, Bill?"

"You could say that, but the facts are causing it. Look, young Tip and I have beavered away today. Louis Packard was a rep, as you know, and like a lot of his breed he was a pretty fly bird. Lots of irons in lots of fires and always knew somebody who could supply whatever he wanted at the right price and so on. So much we know from talking to his colleagues. He has a decent house—

23

a post-war one out near Theydon Bois—on a mortgage with an endowment. He's had it for twelve years. As you can imagine, the price he paid wasn't as high as prices are today, and so his mortgage, compared with that of most couples, is comparatively small."

"So no money worries to make him disappear?"

"Far from it. He has a banking account—two, in fact, current and deposit—entirely in his own name. Both are very healthy, and his bank manager was quite ready to tell me that neither has had a penny drawn out of them since Packard disappeared."

"Anywhere else he could get money from?"

"Two sources. Building Society and joint account at the bank. His Building Society passbook is in the house—he obviously didn't carry it around with him—and that has over seven thousand in it that hasn't been touched for over a year. His wife says he put his sales bonuses into it and left them there to mount up. She said he was aiming to get ten thousand to invest in some high-return bond or other."

"Sounds like a wise and thrifty man. What about the joint account?"

"He hasn't drawn on that, either. He never has done apparently. His missus gets her monthly salary paid into it, and he used to sweeten it with two hundred and fifty every pay day. That was to cover the mortgage, endowment and quarterly bills."

"No housekeeping—food and whatnot?"

"Ah! Young Tip was on to that. She questioned the wife, who got a bit cagey about it. Her replies weren't satisfactory, George, but this isn't a case, you know. Tip couldn't crack the whip and demand to know things, but she got the impression that Packard was one of those chaps who always had a plentiful supply of ready cash in his pocket out of which to pay the week's grocery bill and buy the booze."

"Which sounds as if he was on to some sort of ready cash fiddle or moonlighting."

"Or both."

"Any idea what?"

Green shook his head. "We haven't had time to go into that sort of thing yet. But we have looked into the business of the car."

"Any joy?"

"You always say negative results are useful."

Masters nodded.

"The road fund is out of date. Has been for fourteen weeks, but according to the computer, nobody has renewed it. So the car is either stuck away somewhere out of sight, or it's running around unlicensed."

"Ah!"

"I thought you'd find all that indicative of something."

"I do. From the way you describe him, Packard isn't the sort not to realize on a valuable car if he no longer has use for it. But if Packard has sold it, the new owner would register the change and, presumably, would have paid the road fund when it was due. On the other hand, if Packard were still wanting to use the car he wouldn't fail to renew the licence, because if he did. . . ."

"Any copper on the beat could pick him up at any time and ask awkward questions Packard wouldn't want to be asked."

"Quite."

"So what do you assume, George?"

"On the face of it, one of two things. Packard is either dead or lying seriously disabled somewhere, or he has lost his memory."

"If he'd lost his memory," countered Green, "at least the car would have turned up somewhere. And if he'd been injured in a crash, well, again the car would figure, even if it were a write off."

"True."

"And we were on to the loss of memory bit straight away. It's the obvious enquiry to make. I got our own Missing Persons people on to it. They've been using the computer, too. Nowhere in the country is there a loss-of-memory case of Packard's description. That's not to say he isn't one of those cases that haven't come to the attention of police or doctors but, hell, George, a chap has to earn his bread somehow, and no employer would take on a man with no papers and no remembered past."

"True. What about the DHSS? Has he asked for relief or benefit anywhere?"

"Newcastle said they thought not, but it was an off-the-cuff answer. They say they'll make a more thorough search, but you know that lot, they'll pay out half a dozen times to the same bloke if he goes to different offices and uses a different name each time. Their operation is too big for this sort of enquiry if you're in a hurry."

Masters sat still for a moment, elbows resting on each side of the chair, half empty glass in one hand and expired pipe in the other. Then he said: "Sum it all up for me, Bill. What do you think I should tell Anderson in the morning?"

"Packard was a man who was pretty keen on money. If he were free and in his right mind he wouldn't have forsaken a valuable house property more than half paid for, a sizeable Building Society account and two healthy bank accounts. That's point one, and you'll notice I'm not talking about leaving a wife he was supposedly fond of and a well-paid job which these days is a sizeable asset.

"Point two is the car. We should be able to trace it, but we can't. That suggests something more than just a husband wanting a change of bed-mate. Talking of which, we have not been able to establish that there was another woman."

"But there could be?"

"Yes. But though we got enough hints about clandestine financial deals and so forth, there was no hint of womanizing. His only passion, apart from his wife, it seems, was tinkering about with cars. He liked doing a bit of mechanic's work and he'd got all the tools and a bench and so on. He spent every weekend at it if he wasn't running his missus around in the car."

"A fairly common and innocuous hobby, then?"

"I reckon we can say that on balance he didn't go off with another woman."

Masters nodded his agreement.

"So," continued Green, "all the hints and clues that might lead us to him, were he alive, are missing. And so is the car. That leads me to one conclusion, and that is that both he and the car are dead. By that I mean they are probably together in the bottom of some lake somewhere."

"An accident that wasn't witnessed?"

"That's the most likely. But he could have been pushed, of course, though there's nothing to suggest he was."

Masters got up to refill the glasses.

"Bill, your experience of such things is better than mine. Tell me how long a submerged car—with or without occupation—is likely to remain undiscovered in this country? Days, years, for ever?"

"Statistics, you mean?"

"Yes."

"As far as I know, there aren't any. But I'd have said, talking from memory, that there are very few places where a car would remain undetected for long. Start with the sea. All our coasts are tidal. Any car that goes in, even if over a cliff, only goes a few yards out at the most, and the next low tide will as like as not uncover it. Rivers? Those that are deep enough to hide a car are navigable and the obstruction would soon be found. The same goes for canals. Lakes usually shelve gently so a vehicle wouldn't get far enough in to cover itself. The exceptions are places like brick-pits and quarries. Very deep with precipitous sides and as like as not in the middle of nowhere and no longer worked. But don't get me wrong. People can and do drown in motor cars in all these places."

"I know, Bill. What I asked you was how long such a tragedy is likely to go undiscovered?"

Green accepted his drink. "I'd have said a matter of

days at the most, except for quarries and the like. Oh, and probably some deep-sided Scottish lochs."

"So you reckon we can say the chances of his having been drowned in such a way and not found after six or seven months are fairly slim?"

Green slurped off the top of his tankard of beer. "That's my opinion, George."

"So what's the total deal that I can hand to Anderson?"

"My nose says he's dead. Probably came to a sticky end. Not suicide, otherwise the car would have come to light. As it hasn't, I think the car has been ringed."

"Couldn't Packard have ringed it himself?"

"He could, of course. He could even have exported it. We'll try Customs at ports tomorrow if you like, to see whether it has gone out of the country under its own numberplates."

"Try that, please."

"Before or after you speak to Anderson?"

"Before. I'll wait until twelve before I ask to see him."

"Fair enough. This isn't bad ale, George. What is it?"

"The usual. Ruddles."

A minute or two later, Wanda and Doris joined them. "All ready, darling," reported Wanda.

"Thank you."

"Got the problem solved, have you?"

"No. In fact my guess is that we've just started it."

"Can you tell us over supper?"

While they ate, the two men told the story to their wives. They were as far as the strawberries and ice cream when Doris said: "I used to meet what were called commercial travellers in my day. Quite a lot in the shop where I worked. As you'd expect, some of them were very nice men. Some were just the opposite. But they all had something in common."

"What was that, love?"

"I don't know how you'd describe it. But they had to be able to go where they weren't wanted, if you know what I mean."

"A bit insensitive, like?" suggested her husband.

"Something like that. If they couldn't push in or stand being rejected, they didn't succeed, and if they didn't succeed, they didn't sell enough, and if they didn't sell enough, they didn't last."

"Go on, please, Doris," said Masters quietly.

Doris reddened at the attention being paid to her. "Well, I mean . . . well, Mr Packard was successful, wasn't he? Obviously, I mean. He'd got a good job, house, plenty of money, wife and all the other things you've spoken of, so I'd say he wasn't the timid, nervous type who would commit suicide."

"Quite right, love," said her husband. "Too sure of himself to want to rob himself of his own presence."

"You can laugh about it. . . ."

"I'm agreeing with you, love."

"Oh. Well . . . and you don't think it's another woman and he was too fond of his worldly goods to leave them behind, so I think you're right to say something beyond his own control has happened to him."

Wanda was full of approval for this unaccustomed intervention on the part of the older woman. "Tell us what you think has happened to him," she urged. "Something drastic beyond his own control, you said, Doris."

"Drastic is right, Wanda, because if he's not in any hospital for treatment, either for injury or loss of memory, which he isn't, or the car would have turned up, then where is he? If he wouldn't voluntarily leave the other things behind, I mean?" She turned to Masters. "I think he must be dead, George. And if he'd died properly. . . ."

"Properly, love?" queried Green.

"You know what I mean. Of an illness or a road accident or something like that."

"I see."

"Well, you'd know about it, wouldn't you? Or his family would. There'd have been an inquest."

"Quite right, Doris," said Masters.

"What are you going to do about it, darling?" asked Wanda.

"Report to Edgar and let him handle it from then on.

29

Should he decide to start an investigation, he'll first have to decide whereabouts in the country he thinks Packard could have disappeared, because it will be the responsibility of the force in that area to do the work."

Green grimaced. "Who's going to be able to decide where he went missing? Edgar Anderson can't order other Constabularies to undertake enquiries."

"Maybe not. But we have a liaison officer at the Home Office, and the Home Secretary can order any force to investigate. Then there's Top Cop. . . ."

"Top Cop?" asked Doris.

"Inspector General," said her husband. "The senior bobby in the kingdom."

"Coffee everybody?" asked Wanda.

2

Anderson was quite adamant.

"This whole thing is getting out of hand. I've had my wife harassing me for heaven knows how long and now, after I reluctantly asked you to put the lid on it for me, you come up with all this rigmarole. I'm not going to try to find some other force to send on a wild goose chase. That car was stolen—if stolen is the right word, which I very much doubt—in the Metropolitan area. And as the loss of the car seems to be the only basis for a police enquiry, we here, in the Met, will do it. More specifically, you will do it. Moreover, you will not waste time. You will get down to it immediately and either show there is no case to investigate or, if there is, wrap it up in double quick time. Is that understood?"

Masters, feeling somewhat aggrieved that Anderson should adopt such an attitude after he himself had instigated the chain of events which had led to this meeting, merely nodded. He preferred not to speak lest any comment he should make might be undiplomatic. Not from the work point of view. This enquiry, case, or whatever it eventually turned out to be, was just another bit of work. Not that. His reticence was occasioned by the knowledge that Anderson would be feeling mighty uncomfortable at being forced into a corner by his wife and by having, in order to satisfy her demand, to use a leading team among his crime staff for the purpose. Masters knew that Anderson was both ashamed and annoyed at the nepotism he was showing by—quite rightly—not resisting Beryl's demands firmly and finally.

"I asked if that was understood, George?"

"Perfectly, sir. I know we neither of us like having been manoeuvred into this position but, for my part, I shall forget the circumstances that have brought us to this point, and though I shall keep an open mind about the case, I shall treat it extremely seriously."

"And expeditiously."

"As expeditiously as whatever we turn up demands."

"If you turn anything up."

"I think, sir, that one way or another, we must get to the bottom of the affair—for your sake."

Anderson had the grace to grin. "You know Beryl, George. Over something like this she's like one of those old Staffordshire fighting dogs. Once her teeth have closed on it neither hell nor high water will make her let go."

Masters got to his feet. "In that case, sir, I'll keep you constantly informed so that you can report progress to Mrs Anderson daily."

"Get out," retorted Anderson. "I can do without your mock sympathy."

A few minutes later, Masters was in his office, having called his team together for briefing.

"Bill," he said, "you and Tip have done a lot of the useful spadework. Enough, that is, to suggest we have a case, but unless it is a serious matter we are looking into, I can't see that the likes of us have any business to be investigating it. I propose, therefore, to accord it the degree of importance that our being involved warrants. We shall treat it as murder."

"Understand the thinking," agreed Green, "and you already know what I think about it."

"What's that?" demanded Berger, who so far had not been involved.

"Tell him, Bill, please."

Green briefed Berger, with occasional help from Tip, while Masters added the gist of his conversation with Anderson.

"Now we are all in the picture. Bill, I'd like you and Berger to go and see Packard's employers officially. I don't need to tell you what we want."

"Everything," grunted Green. "I've been thinking it over, George, so I reckon I know what I'm after, having met one or two of his mates. There's just one thing, though."

"What's that?"

"We may get a good bit of what we want to know from Packard's managers at the company office, but to get to know most about him we'll want to talk to reps from other companies that he met in the field. The chaps he met at nights in the pubs where these characters stay. And that's where we'll find 'em. Out in the field. We might have to dig deep to uncover his murky past."

"If he's got one," said Berger.

"Don't start getting defeatist, lad," said Green.

Masters got to his feet. "It's latish for lunch already. Stick close to home this afternoon, Bull. Then tomorrow if the need arises, we can get out and about. Tip and I will interview his wife again. Tip, you might phone her and say we hope to be with her by three o'clock."

"Right, sir. And a car?"

"Yes, please. Ours. Berger, you get a pool vehicle."

"Don't do yourselves too badly, do you?" said Green as he sank into the low, armless chair alongside the coffee table in the sales director's office. "All home comforts."

"Anybody can be uncomfortable."

The sales director, Cecil Emery, gave his little Public Relations laugh as he said this, and gestured for Berger to take a seat, too. "I can have mini-conferences here, without having to occupy one of the larger meeting rooms. I can get a relaxed atmosphere."

"When you're carpeting people, you mean?"

Emery was plump, overly well-dressed and highly perfumed. He hitched his trousers at the knees as he too sat down.

"Fortunately that doesn't often happen. I pride myself

on being able to choose good material for my field force. They spearhead the selling side of the company, and we are highly successful. Ah! Here's coffee. Thank you, Melinda, I'll have it here."

When the secretary had stationed the brassy looking trolley at his elbow and left the office, Emery got to his feet. "The trouble with these things," he said, as he twisted the lid of a giant thermos until a green flag showed in the little aperture above the spout, "is that you have to stand up to work them. The other thing is, you can't hold a cup on its saucer under the flow. Just the cup itself. See!" He pressed the large white-metal plate at the top, and coffee flowed into the cup. "Help yourself to milk and sugar."

"You even have company crockery," said Green, examining the cup. "Crest and name."

"It helps," said Emery. "Everything helps. All publicity, that is. Members of the firm are impressed, and visitors, to see the name ALPURPLAS on things like our cups as well as on letterheads and envelopes. It gives an air of success. Nothing succeeds like success, you know."

"So I'm learning," said Green, helping himself to one of the biscuits from the plate. "And you've got a good mixture here, too. I'm rather partial to these little wafers." He looked up at Emery. "Packard," he said, changing his tone. "Tell me about him."

"What, specifically?"

"Specifically everything. You people keep Gestapo dossiers on all your employees, don't you?"

"Personnel files, yes."

"That's what you call them, is it? So what can you tell me about him other than the fact that he was a rep?"

"He wasn't a rep, actually."

"No? What do you call travellers these days? Sales executives or commercial operatives or some such?"

"No, we call them reps. But Packard was a District Manager."

"Meaning what?"

"Meaning that we divide the country into districts, each district embodying several reps' territories. Every district has a manager who is responsible for the reps on the various territories comprising that district."

"And they come directly under you?"

Emery shook his head. "I have two Area Controllers as my immediate contacts. Each is responsible for the districts in his half of the UK. Packard reported directly to the Eastern Area Controller, Harvey Collett."

"They work here, in the office?"

"Partly. They have offices in this building, but I insist that they, too, get out and about among their people most of the time. District Managers are out the whole time, of course, chasing up their people, and even taking over the territories of reps who are ill or on holiday." Emery leant forward. "Lots of firms expect their reps to come back to the front office to report every Friday. I don't. I want my people beavering away on their patches, selling the products. Their reports are collected by the DMs and their instructions handed to them in the battle line. Their time isn't wasted driving in here to London every week, wasting petrol and missing sales calls."

Berger said: "If you never see your reps, they—and their District Managers—could be fooling you rotten, couldn't they?"

Emery laughed. "I watch it," he said. "Reps have to report every call they make. There's an absolute weekly minimum, which I'll accept just once or twice. At other times I expect the minimum to be exceeded."

"Even if they sell nothing on a call."

"We accept that a customer won't always buy. We allow a few abortive calls."

"What's to stop the reps putting a few bogus non-successful calls in their reports—just to make up the numbers you demand?"

"Two things. When I say we accept a few abortive calls, I mean a very few, so at best they couldn't hit more than one of them a week. That's the first safeguard. The

35

second is the knowledge that we here, in the office, ring every customer who is listed as having been visited but who hasn't bought."

"To check up that the rep is telling the truth?"

"Oh, we do it diplomatically. We don't ask straight out if the rep called. We say he has asked us to ring because when he called last Thursday he forgot to tell them of a new product or a new sales offer. Something like that. If he wasn't there last Thursday the customer always lets you know, one way or another."

"I haven't seen him for a month or some such?"

"That's it. The reps know better than to try it on, because there's no second chance."

"The sack?" grunted Green.

"Without ceremony."

"I'm surprised you've got a field force."

"Why?"

"Treating them that way."

"Ah, we treat them very well. Very well indeed. We pay them over the odds, and we reward success very highly. It's cheaper to do that than to keep a lower-paid, inefficient team in the field."

"And I suppose you make sure all your salesmen are efficient by giving them high-powered training courses with a lot of rizz-bum-ra to rouse their enthusiasm."

Emery looked at Green pityingly. "That doesn't sell the products. I told you, I don't take my team off their patches for high-powered training sessions. The DMs have little meetings of their own six or seven reps perhaps once a month. But only to introduce them to a new range or to discuss other matters that come up. No, Mr Green, my people are proven and trained salesmen before I sign them on. It's cheaper to poach successful people from other companies than to go to all the expense of having training teams, training rooms, costly training gadgets and learner reps living the life of Riley in some nearby hotel for six weeks while one tries to instill the business of selling into them, only to find they fall short of one's standards in the end."

Green grunted. "How do you know which chap to poach?"

Emery grinned. "My field force is my team of head-hunters. Among the great brotherhood of reps there's a vast knowledge of each others' prowess. They meet in hotels every night, bump into each other in shops and pubs, pick up all manner of gossip and generally know what goes on in their areas. They can smell the successful rep almost by instinct, from watching orders being posted at night, from the solid assurance that success evinces, from the eagerness which good reps show in the mornings, the way they keep their cars and their clothes. In their own line of business, and by that I mean selling generally, reps are pretty canny and not easily hood-winked by brashness and the bravado some salesmen assume to cover up their doubtful professional qualities."

Green took out a crumpled packet of Kensitas and extracted a cigarette carefully. "That means you poached Packard from some other firm."

"That's right. About five and a half years ago. From a pharmaceutical company. Drug reps are good people to get hold of, because their firms are obliged to train them highly for obvious reasons. In fact, the Association of British Pharmaceutical Industries has a universal reps' exam. A sort of degree course in practical selling, you might call it. A rep who makes the grade in that field for a number of years could well be a good prospect for the likes of us."

"Even though he's a specialist in selling drugs which, I take it, don't figure among your products."

"A good rep is a good rep whether he's selling raspberry jam or spare parts for aeroplanes."

Berger asked: "What exactly do you make and sell, Mr Emery?"

"Our name, ALPURPLAS, is a shortened form of ALL-PURPOSE-PLASTICS."

"Kitchen-ware and stuff like that?"

Emery shook his head. "All purpose is a mistake. We do more of the high-class stuff. For electrics and electronics, plane and car engines, special mouldings, superior materials . . . you can visualize what I mean, but we're not above producing the more domestic type of article. Not washing-up bowls, exactly. But we produce a black sack, for instance, for packing expensive export goods, which is roughly a hundred times as strong as the one the dustman leaves at your house every week. Then there's rigid glazing, shatterproof and bulletproof, and we make special cloches for horticultural research establishments. Some of them are very sophisticated and very large indeed. In fact, we produce hundreds of stock items and even more specials."

"I'm impressed," grunted Green. "You've spent a long time telling me how efficient you are and how economically-minded you are, but something doesn't add up."

"No? What's that?"

"Why you didn't report Packard's car as stolen when he first disappeared. Yet you have now made just that complaint. I would have thought you would have bust a gut to get five or six thousand pounds' worth of car back. Unless you've claimed insurance on it?"

"No insurance claim," said Emery. "Insurers won't pay out unless you report the car to the police as having been stolen."

"Why no action to recover the loss?"

"It's as I told you. We treat members of our field force very well indeed. We demand a lot of them, but we give a lot in return, like not embarrassing them or their families by accusing them of stealing motor cars. I'd rather write the thing off than accuse Packard of theft when I'm morally certain that he has not willingly stolen it and that he is, himself, in some mental or physical trouble somewhere. When Mrs Packard rang me to say that the only way to get you people to take an interest in the man's disappearance was to claim that there was a criminal act involved, I agreed to say that the missing car had been stolen, together with lots of other things our reps are accustomed to carrying with them. So I informed the police that we had suffered loss by theft to the tune of nearly ten thousand pounds as well as certain secret or semi-secret specifications. That seems to have gingered things up a bit, and here you are, taking an interest within twenty-four hours."

"You said you think Packard is in mental or physical trouble. Why that, and not that he's just decamped with some bird?"

"You wouldn't ask that if you knew Packard. Basically he's got a hide like a rhinoceros and he's as selfish—or self-seeking—as hell. I don't say he wouldn't try to pull any birds he fancied. He would. But only to use them. He'd never let one interfere with his own interests. He was on the way up, and he knew it. He came to us from his previous job because we offered him more—better money, better car, better prospects. In less than three years he achieved his present status of District Manager. Within another two he'd have become an Area Controller. He knew that. In fact I told him so myself. As a rep he won all the individual prizes. As a DM his district won all the team prizes, and those against all the odds."

"What odds?"

"His area hadn't got the population and industry to make the money other more industrial areas have. East Anglia, with those parts of Essex that are outside the boundaries of London proper. It's considered a graveyard for selling. One person and one cow per acre! But Packard made it pay. The new research and manufacturing facilities in Cambridge, the growth of Norwich both in population and industry . . . he was on to them all. Do you know he'd even started us up on producing a much stronger sort of black bag for container planting among horticulturalists, growers and garden centres? He just about created the need where none existed. The new bag greatly lessened losses by tearing and it was designed with loops to be easier to handle. All that sort of thing. He sold scores of thousands of pounds' worth of those. He got an award for it. Now those bags are sold all over the country and we even export a small number. No, he'd got too much to lose to absent himself willingly, and he knew it."

"And you'd told him there was to be promotion in the foreseeable future?"

"As long as he continued the good work and kept his nose clean. Why do you ask?"

"There might be somebody who thought he was on the way to stepping into their shoes."

"Oh, I see. Somebody who might want him out of the way, you mean?" Emery shook his head. "Nothing like that. He knew—and everybody else involved knew—that we were going to diversify. That the plans were already made in outline. Part of planning is to decide whether you've got the right personnel to carry out your plans. One of my Area Controllers was earmarked for starting up a second, smaller field force. Packard was to take over his job. It is quite simple, really. We've got to the stage where we've too many products for each individual man to handle properly. You can't actively sell many lines in a customer call that lasts only a few minutes. So some are getting neglected. They need a bit of pushing in their own right. We've decided the way to do it is to farm some of them out to a second, subsidiary sales force. With a different name, of course. Customers won't see reps from the same company twice in one week."

"I think I've got all that," murmured Green. "And what I've heard from you strengthens the belief that Packard has suffered a nasty of some sort."

"I said mental or physical. I didn't mean mental, not unless he's suffered injury to the brain. I'm no expert, of course, but, as I've indicated, mentally, Louis Packard was as tough as old boots. There was no fine edge in his mental make-up. Of the earth, earthy, you might say. Practical, confident, solid, and woe betide anybody who got in his way."

"Quarrelsome sort of bloke, was he?" asked Berger.

"Not that I know of. If you spat in his ale he would be too clever to spit in yours, but the next time you used that same bar there'd be cyanide in your pint. And, as like as not, he'd be there to ask you if you were feeling unwell after you'd downed it. Just to let you know, before the end, that he'd got his own back."

"Nice chap," murmured Berger.

"He was," asserted Emery. "If he wasn't crossed."

Green sat up. "I reckon we've got his character now. Just one or two other things, Mr Emery. Let's assume the worst for a moment. That he's dead, although the same applies if he's suffering from loss of memory."

"What do you mean?"

"Ways of identifying the body. Did he wear a ring, for instance? Any noticeable scars? That sort of thing."

"No ring and no scars that I knew of. But I expect he'd be wearing a gold watch. We presented him with one a year last December for general good work. Not an earned bonus, you understand. Come Christmas each year we hand out four or five gifts to field force members. A stereo, say, or a watch or a camera."

"Any inscription on the watch?"

"None. But it's exactly the same as this. Strap and all." Emery took the watch and its expanding bracelet from his wrist and handed it to Green.

"Valuable, I suppose?"

"Extremely. We go in for good things."

Green noted the make and handed the watch over to Berger for inspection.

"Number Seventeen, The Crescent, sir," said Tip, expertly drawing the large Rover to a halt outside one of a row of semi-detached houses. Masters thanked her and looked about him. Less than a hundred yards back they had passed a private school for girls. Obviously a thriving school, but not custom-built: one that had grown and prospered over the years. The nucleus, as far as he could judge, had been two large, adjoining Victorian houses, four storeys high. Little brick and glass bridges joined the two at bottom and top. And then there were later additions. What looked like a hall or gymnasium, in newish, raw brick had been tacked on at one end, while at the other, in place of a third house had been built a mini-tower block in concrete alongside which was a cycle shed. There was no all-enclosing fence. Instead, each of the original property walls had been left standing: different heights, different building materials and different gateways, at each of which the school authorities had seen fit to erect a large green board bearing the name of the school and its badge. He had glimpsed one or two of the pupils. Obviously girls from a quite young age up to eighteen were catered for. Masters had noted with some satisfaction that all were in a school summer uniform—shoes, white socks on bare legs, print dresses and green blazers with straw hats. To his eye they looked wholesome—fat, thin, tall, short, bespectacled, freckled—the usual mixture, but without sloppy fashion shoes, nylons, punk hair and all the other ghastlies he had become accustomed to seeing on schoolgirls.

Other large houses had been divided into flats. All cared for and pleasantly curtained. Some had obviously been knocked down, to make way for a serried jumble of little bungalows, each with a shallow ramp up to an unusually wide front door. Special provision for the disabled, he guessed—special and pleasant provision, with little undivided gardens with flower beds and handkerchief-sized lawns.

The little row of semis, again apparently built on the site of several demolished houses, still looked new. The trees indicated this. New houses on new sites don't usually have gardens in which grow broadleaved trees, full of years.

"The neighbourhood looks fairly prosperous," said Masters.

"It is, sir," said Tip confidently. "Good quality curtains everywhere and the baby's pram two doors back is an expensive one. Besides, look at the paintwork."

Masters grinned. It was a new experience for him to have the benefit of a woman's observations when on a case. He and the other men would never have noticed the quality of the curtains or known the provenance of a pram.

Ida Packard answered the door.

"My name is Masters. You've already met Detective Sergeant Tippen. You were expecting us I believe, Mrs Packard?"

"This morning, actually, otherwise I wouldn't have had a full day off work. Just half a day. It's upset my flexi-time credit."

As Masters followed her into the hallway and then into the sitting room of the house he tried to sum her up. Thirty-fivish, he supposed, with an attractive figure that would, he reckoned, stay pretty much the same until old age. The face was not thin, but spare-fleshed, very tanned and taut, with none of the pleasant roundness of contours of chin and cheekbones that he himself preferred. Nor of the mouth. It was too much of a thin red line. And the voice that came out of it! There was no noticeable accent that he could place as coming from any particular area, merely a harshness that suggested it had been cultivated from a higher-pitched whine that had needed to be carefully nurtured if it was not to slip back to its original timbre.

"Why were you expecting us this morning, Mrs Packard?" Masters took the armchair she had indicated.

"Because my aunt—she's sort of second cousin really, and the wife of your Assistant Commissioner, you know—rang me at eight o'clock to say she had arranged for you to come straight away and I was to be here to see you. So I had to make some very quick arrangements to be off work today. I'm a Section Leader in the Computer Information Department in our company, and making hurried re-arrangements for five or six staff is not all that easy."

"I see. Unfortunately, Mrs Anderson does not give me any orders direct. The AC (Crime) does that, and he realizes, like you, that hurried re-arrangements of duties can often take time. So this afternoon was the earliest we could get along to see you."

43

Ida Packard turned the corners of her mouth down to make the complaint. "That's what the police always do. They're dilatory. I've found that out since my husband disappeared. They're never willing to do anything."

Tip, who had taken a seat on the sofa in the window, came into the conversation at this point. "Mrs Packard," she said. "I'm not suggesting that you have ever thought of leaving your husband, but just supposing you had decided to do so for some reason—because he was unkind to you, or played around with other women, or because you yourself wanted to live with another man—would you expect the police to come harassing you? I don't think you would, you know, because adult citizens are free agents, and so long as no law is broken, they can come and go as they please."

"But Louis could be hurt or in danger."

"There is that possibility. But the police and medical cover in this country is such that he could seek protection or help whatever had happened. And then we should know about it. Your husband has not sought medical help anywhere as far as we can determine, and he certainly hasn't abandoned his car anywhere as a pointer to his actions or activities."

"You're saying he went away deliberately? Planned it?"

"It's a possibility, you must admit."

"I don't admit it. He would never deliberately leave me."

"In that case," said Masters, "let us get down to seeing what we can do to find him. First of all, Mrs Packard, have you a recent photograph of your husband? A good likeness?"

She got to her feet, and from a small bureau in the corner of the room fetched one of the modern photograph albums that contain two or three dozen flip-over plastic envelopes. "There must be at least a dozen of Louis in there, and we only got it about a year ago, so they should be up-to-date."

"Would you point them out to Sergeant Tippen and, if possible, give us the one she chooses as that likely to be the most useful to us?"

While the two women spent some minutes over the photographs Masters, emboldened by the fact that there were a number of ashtrays about the room, some showing signs of current use, took out the brassy tin of Warlock Flake and started to pack his pipe. While doing so, he looked about him. The room was well furnished in a modern style and, Masters guessed, quite expensively. They were all there, the colour television, the video, room dividers carrying good-quality knick-knacks, mostly of cut glass, a largish unit against one wall, built up to take books, tapes, records, drink and all manner of *objets d'art* which, though not to his liking, proclaimed that money had been spent lavishly. He found it arid, unhomely, proclaiming too much pride of possession for his taste. He supposed the lack of children robbed it of appeal. He was reminded of the story of the little daughter of a diplomat who, throughout the first eight or nine years of her life, had been shunted round the various capitals of the world, never staying long enough in one place to put down any roots. When finally her father was posted back to England, the inevitable search for accommodation had begun. A friendly grown-up had remarked to the little girl how difficult it was proving for her father and mother to find a home, to which the little girl had replied gravely, "Oh, we've got a home. All we want now is a house to put it in."

"I've got the photograph, sir," said Tip, "and a description of the clothes Mr Packard was wearing at the time he left the house."

"And what he might have had in his case?"

"I don't understand?"

"Did he go off wearing a blue suit, with a grey one in his bag, for instance?"

"Oh, sorry, sir."

"Mrs Packard?"

"Louis used to take just the one suit with him. He alternated each week, of course, and he aways carried jeans and a sports shirt for evenings."

Masters accepted this fact without comment, but it

45

sounded as though Packard, after the day's work, had not usually been content to stay in the hotel where he had booked a room, but had dressed down to get out and about on the town.

"He was last at home on a Sunday, Mrs Packard?"

"Monday morning, actually. We had to get up early on Mondays because he wanted to beat the heavy traffic. He used to get out to the east of London and then stop for breakfast at one of those roadside cafés."

"I see. Did he always go to the same one every Monday morning?"

"Yes. One on the trunk road." She gave them its location.

"And the date of the Monday when you last saw him?"

"November the seventh last year."

"Did he ever telephone you during the working week?"

"Only on Thursday nights."

"Every Thursday?"

"Yes. Well, nearly every Thursday."

"Why Thursday?"

"To tell me what he wanted to do at the weekend or to ask me to make sure I'd got the clothes he'd want ready for him to wear or to ask me to book a table somewhere for dinner on Saturday night. Thousands of things, over the years. Would I get things from motor accessory shops, or nails and screws if he wanted to do something about the house. You know the sort of thing."

"I get the picture, Mrs Packard. Did he ring you on Thursday the tenth of November?"

"No."

"Didn't that worry you?"

"Not really. He nearly always did ring on Thursdays, but he used to say that he might miss if he was pushed."

"Meaning otherwise engaged on business matters?"

"Yes."

"Company business or private?"

He could see he had touched on something. Just a faint look of fear or maybe even anger in the eyes. The

46

mouth straightened its line. "He wasn't in the habit of chasing other women if that's what you're hinting at."

"I wasn't hinting, I was asking. When men leave home it is often because of another woman, and it's equally often said that the wife is the last to know."

"I wouldn't be. When my husband came home on a Friday I had to be ready to be his wife. And on Saturday and Sunday, too. I'd have known all right if there had been other women."

"Thank you. I'll accept that. But there are other types of private business. Transactions of one sort or another which, though probably not illegal, are best kept quiet."

She was on the defensive. "If there were, I don't know anything about them."

Tip asked. "Did he never bring home things for you or the house? Blouses or tights, perhaps? Or a food mixer or bottles of spirits?"

"Well of course, he did bring me things home. Little presents. All husbands do."

Masters glanced at Tip to warn her not to pursue the subject. Instead, he himself said: "We were informed that your husband seemed always to have a large supply of ready cash with which to pay household bills, even large bills like electricity and telephone."

"What if he did?"

"It is a little unusual. I'm interested in the unusual. It could well give me a pointer as to your husband's whereabouts."

"How?"

"I don't know—yet. But I have to consider that Mr Packard might have fallen foul of somebody with whom he had been doing clandestine business deals."

"He always knew where he could get things. . . ."

"Cheaply, you mean?"

"He met reps of every other company. Got to know them. They all let their friends have things at reasonable rates."

"Wholesale, you mean?"

"Yes. But he didn't get all that many. You can look round if you like. Just a few cast-iron dishes and pans for the kitchen. That sort of thing."

"And clothing for you?" asked Tip shrewdly.

"What if he did? Wouldn't any man in his position get his wife a few nice things for her holidays?"

"I'm sure he would," agreed Masters, "but that doesn't explain your husband always having in his possession a large amount of money in notes."

"What are you trying to do?" demanded Mrs Packard. "Incriminate my husband or find him?"

"Incriminate him? In what way?" asked Masters.

"All these questions about the money he carried in his pocket."

"If the money was come by honestly, and any deals Mr Packard did were strictly legal, as you assert they were, the question of incrimination does not arise. But please don't forget that the only reason we have for interesting ourselves in your husband's disappearance is that there has ostensibly been a crime connected with it. Namely, that somebody has robbed Mr Packard's employers of a valuable motor car and some equally valuable contents. So I suggest you forget any accusations of our attempting to incriminate him and tell me where the ready money came from."

Mrs Packard's mouth grew thinner than ever. "He always drew his expenses in cash."

"Ah! you mean that to keep his float of a hundred pounds up to its proper level he drew cash from the firm to cover what he paid out."

"Yes."

"How often?"

"What do you mean?"

"How often did he send in his expense account?"

"Every week. And the firm always pays expenses by return. They check them after payment and, if necessary, adjust on the next one. That's so the reps aren't kept waiting for their money."

48

"That seems a very good system, but I would like to clarify this business just a little more."

"How do you mean?"

"Your husband was away from home four nights each week?"

"Yes."

"So he had to pay hotel bills for accommodation and food for those four nights, and, presumably, other bills for customer entertainment and his own lunches."

"That's right."

"A hundred pounds wouldn't cover all that for a week."

"Of course it didn't. He just signed the bills for his overnight stays and they were sent to the firm by the hotel managers."

"Thank you. At least we've got a pointer, I think."

"How do you make that out?"

"We can discover from his company's finance department which was the last hotel bill they settled on his behalf. Something which should have been followed up soon after his disappearance, I would have thought. Didn't it occur to you, Mrs Packard?"

The woman frowned. "I did think of it."

"With what result?"

"The company said they got no hotel bills that week. The last one was for the Thursday night before Louis went missing and he came home for the weekend after that."

"So it would seem he went missing on the Monday, before he could book in a hotel."

"Well, yes. That's what I thought, but. . . ."

"But what, Mrs Packard?"

"It seemed. . . ."

"Seemed what?" asked Masters quietly.

"Too easy," she whispered.

"Your husband played some sort of game with hotel bills, did he? Were you worried that if enquiries were pressed too closely into his stays at certain hotels, irregularities might come to light? Was that why it was too easy to assume he had disappeared on the Monday?"

"I don't know what he did," she answered. "There are perks to repping just as there are to any other job, but I never asked him what they were or anything about them."

"Yet you suspect they were responsible for his ever-ready flow of cash without his having to draw it from the bank and you also suspect that the perk—if that's what you like to call it—was connected with his hotel bills. Am I right?"

"I've told you I don't know."

"I think you have told me anyway, Mrs Packard. If his money had come from a bit of buying and selling on the side you would have told me so, because there's nothing basically criminal in that, though the Inland Revenue might consider it illegal not to declare figures for such trading. But bill fixing could be fraud, and fraud is a crime."

"I've said I don't know what you're talking about and I'm going to complain about you to my aunt."

"Fine. You can also tell Mrs Anderson that I shall be repeating my suspicions in an official report to Mr Anderson. In that way, they'll both know."

"I've got it all down in shorthand, Mrs Packard," said Tip. "Every word. So there won't be any mistakes."

"How clever of you."

"Not at all. Just the usual service."

Ida Packard turned to Masters. "I honestly don't know whether Louis got up to any fun and games with hotel bills. But just in case he had, I didn't push Alpurplas too hard to investigate that bit. You see, at first I thought he'd come back. After a few days or weeks maybe, and I didn't want him getting home to find I'd forced his bosses into sniffing out something he would want to keep under cover."

"I understand," said Masters sympathetically. "And I suppose that as the weeks went by and your husband did not return you found it was too late to start pressing

Alpurplas to put private detectives on to investigating the hotels the firm's records showed him as having used?"

She nodded miserably.

"But you really do want him back?"

She nodded again, head low.

"Right. Let's get down to finding him, shall we. How long had he worked for Alpurplas?"

"About five and a half years."

"So he must have had another job before this one. What was it?"

"He was a rep. A pharmaceutical rep."

"A highly respected body of men as a whole, I believe."

"Oh, yes. Mostly degree people and ever so highly trained."

"But your husband left to join Alpurplas?"

"Yes."

"Just a moment, please," requested Tip. "Could I have the name of the pharmaceutical firm your husband worked for, Mrs Packard? For the notes."

"AVL," replied Ida. "Ayre Valley Laboratories. They make a lot of what are known as topical medicines. That's the sort you don't take internally, you know."

"Lotions and drops and ointments?" asked Tip.

"They do others of course. Injections mainly, I think. But some tablets and capsules and powders as well. When Louis worked for them we had our spare room almost full of samples. He's still got a few up in the loft."

"Why did your husband change jobs?" asked Masters.

"Why does anybody change jobs these days? More money, of course."

"And more perks?"

"How do you mean?"

"I've dealt with pharmaceutical firms. Their reps have very small areas. Two or three hundred doctors to each rep, I believe. Something of that order, anyway. And doctors are so thick on the ground that except for the very remote areas, like the Highlands, that number can be found within very easy motoring distance of the house

51

of any rep who lives on his territory. So pharmaceutical reps always work from home. They don't stay in hotels overnight. Am I right?"

"Louis always lived at home then," she admitted. "But I'm not saying he changed so's he could fiddle hotel bills. He got better pay and bonuses with Alpurplas because everything he sold was credited direct to him. The AVL reps didn't actually sell anything. They just recommended stuff and it was the doctors who had to prescribe it and the chemists who had to buy it. Louis said he never got his fair share of bonuses, because all the reps shared equally in the national sales—if they were big enough, that is."

"Thank you for explaining," said Masters. "Now something else. Did Mr Packard have any enemies that you know of?"

She shook her head.

"You're saying he got on like a house on fire with all his colleagues and bosses, both in Alpurplas and AVL?"

"More or less, I think. Of course there were one or two people he didn't think much of. But that's the same for everybody, isn't it?"

"It is, indeed. We all have our likes and dislikes, but I meant something rather more out of the ordinary."

"In what way?"

"Did your husband rouse anybody's jealousy because of his selling skills, perhaps? Had he beaten anybody to some promotion, a fact resented by the beaten person? Had he ever been angry himself about not getting what he considered to be his just dues or promotion? Had he fought with somebody over an argument in a pub or anything like that? Carved somebody up in his car? Had somebody informed on him in a sort of tale-telling manner?"

"About what?"

"About anything. Fiddles, perks, women . . . anything at all. Was he hard on somebody and had him dismissed?"

"I can't think of anything like that involving Louis."

"No? There are very few people in a competitive world who wouldn't want to get rid of somebody from their company or who, themselves, are not the objects of some . . ." Masters shrugged, ". . . not hatred or anger, perhaps, but commercial displeasure, shall we say?"

Ida Packard shook her head vehemently. "There was nothing like that with Louis."

"As far as you know."

In the car on the way back to the Yard, Tip said: "I told you I was a secretary before I joined the force, sir."

"So you did. And very useful the training seems to have been for this job. Your typed memo was very nicely laid out, with no mistakes. Very different from those my previous sergeants have offered up at times. And the shorthand you are obviously quite expert at . . . well, that could be useful, but probably not as much as you think."

"Why not, sir?"

"I prefer members of my team to train their memories towards the goal of total recall."

"But, sir, shorthand *is* total recall."

"No, Tip, it isn't. It is an accurate note of what is said. But it makes no mention of circumstances. If you rely on shorthand, you'll probably do an excellent job of reading it back to us at our report sessions, but you won't be telling us whether the person talking was weeping, patently sincere, shifty-eyed, shuffling cards, doddling or limping on a sprained ankle at the time. And circumstances often tell us more than words spoken."

Tip seemed a little downcast as she changed gears determinedly and caused the big car to accelerate away with a jerk.

"Don't get upset about things," counselled Masters. "You've only been with us a couple of days. You must expect to take a little time to settle in to our ways."

"I know, sir," wailed Tip, "but I seem to have done everything wrong, don't I? I shouldn't have rung Mrs Anderson, I shouldn't have taken shorthand notes, and even Sergeant Berger tells me I'm wrong to call you 'sir.'"

Masters laughed. "None of those things is wrong. Everything you have done has been perfectly correct. Very able, in fact. But when you join a tea.n like ours, you just have to temper your ability to fit in with the chosen way of working."

"Yes, sir."

"When you were taking your secretarial course, I suppose you were taught the modern way of laying out a letter, with a gap between paragraphs and no indentation, with the place for the originator's signature down at the bottom left."

"Yes, sir."

"Did you ever have a boss who preferred his letters to look like letters? With indentations at the start of paras and a place at the bottom right for signing?"

"Yes, sir."

"And you complied, no doubt. In other words you made full use of your typing ability, but you adapted the method you had been taught to satisfy the man who employed you."

"Yes, sir."

"That's what I would like you to do in my firm. Learn as you go along and accept that we have tried and tested ways of doing things, or simply preferences in some cases. As for Sergeant Berger suggesting you should call me 'Chief', that is simply tradition within the team. Strictly speaking, according to police discipline, you should address me as 'sir.' We have this slightly more friendly way of carrying on. I don't want to stop you calling me 'sir' if you prefer it. But if you use 'Chief', you can address me as that, and you can refer to me as that when talking to the others. Far simpler to say, 'The Chief did that' than 'The Chief Superintendent' or 'DCS Masters.' But it's up to you."

"Thank you, sir."

Masters grinned. "You know where I live. Come round for supper tonight. Seven thirty. And bring Berger with you. I'll leave it to you to tell him."

"Right, sir."

The four of them were sitting round the exquisitely laid supper table in the dining room of what Green usually referred to as "Wanda's Palace." Tip had visited the house on a previous occasion, when every surface had been covered with maps and the rooms crowded with people, and so she had not had a fair viewing of how Wanda ran this small house of hers. Now she appreciated it and was slightly overawed, not by the people, all of whom she knew fairly well, but by the table appointments and the gentle style of living.

Tip had also been given a lesson in total recall. She could not judge how exact was the report made by Berger at the supper table of the visit he and Green had made to Cecil Emery, but it seemed fully authentic, while she knew that the account of his interview with Mrs Packard, given by Masters, was so exact as to be almost unbelievable.

"I'll pass it all on to the DCI in the morning, Chief," said Berger after hearing what Masters had to say. "Are there any things you want us to do straight off?"

"Yes, please. Tidy up a bit. Get the make, number and colour of the missing car. Try to discover if there was a known or expected route for Packard to follow that week. Look at the hotel bills after that so that we know the places he usually favoured. Even the garages where he got his petrol. The company will have those bills to authenticate his expenses and for reclaiming VAT, I imagine. I want us to be as fully briefed as possible by lunchtime tomorrow."

"Right, Chief. Report to you in your office at midday?"

"Please. But let me know his route as soon as you can get it. Phone it through. If I'm not there, leave a message."

Berger nodded. "What will you be doing yourself, Chief?"

"Digging a little further back. I don't really know how much I can rely on what Mrs Packard has told me, but I'm inclined to believe her, because it bears out, to some degree at any rate, what you got from this chap Emery."

"In what way, darling?" asked Wanda, who had sat quietly listening throughout the meal, performing her duties as hostess quite unobtrusively.

"That Packard was a skilled man in his line, that he was on the up-and-up and that, ostensibly, he had no great enemies. I say 'ostensibly' advisedly, meaning they were not open or recognizably so, but they were there just the same. In the real world, hard men—and Emery says Packard was an unforgiving man who would make sure he repaid all enmity in full measure—hard men drive opposition underground. It can't be seen, but it is there. For certain. Just as I'm certain that such men put people's backs up, even if only by a sneering word or an uncaring gesture."

"I think—no, I'm sure—I see what you mean, George. Are you also implying that such ill-feeling, driven underground and not allowed to come out into the open to dissolve, seethes and festers, growing worse as time goes by?"

"Until it erupts, yes. The eruption can come like a volcano, because the pressure has built up to a point where it can no longer be contained, or there comes an unexpected but opportune moment when somebody can act to level the score. An opportunity not to be missed, when somebody like Packard makes a mistake at the wrong time, leaving himself vulnerable and open to a stroke of revenge."

Wanda frowned slightly. "It's a good thought. Probably completely tenable, George. But by adopting it you are coming down exclusively on the side of somebody having done Packard a serious mischief, whereas accident of one sort or another may be the cause of his disappearance."

"Quite right, sweetheart. I shouldn't be on this case at all, but seeing that it has been thrust upon me, I propose to tackle it from the point of view of a murder team. There are signs to point me that way. If there had been an accident—physical or mental—involving Packard, I think it would have come to light by now. So, as I

56

prefer a positive approach rather than to be passive—as keeping an open-mind would lead me to be—I propose to assume that Packard is dead, not by his own hand, and treat the case as murder. There is usually motive for murder—where it concerns a mature, strong minded, powerful man like Packard, as opposed to a woman or child who is killed by some deranged rapist or pathological killer. I believe that motive will be revenge—occasioned by hatred or greed or whatever comes between man and man to set them at one another's throats. So I'm going to dig deeper into the past, long enough back to allow for the seething and festering you mentioned to achieve enough head of steam to blow its top. In other words, I'm going to see Packard's previous employers at AVL, to get a picture of him from their point of view. Then I'm going to compare the two pictures we shall have and play that game you sometimes see in newspapers."

"Spot the difference, you mean?"

"That's it. Two drawings with minute differences. A character with three buttons on his jacket in one cartoon and only two buttons in the second. It's worth a try, and I haven't much else to go on."

"It sounds a very good idea to me, darling," said Wanda. " 'Spot the difference.' I wonder how many times we've all played that game?"

3

The Managing Director of AVL was far from happy at the arrival of a high-powered Yard man in his offices. When informed of the presence of Masters and Tip in his foyer his immediate thought—after wondering what he himself might have done wrong—was how would a police investigation, whatever it was about, affect his company. Adversely, of course. So he was feeling far from pleased when he growled through the internal line, "Send them up. No! *Bring* them up. My PA will meet you at the fourth-floor lifts."

"How can I help you, Mr Masters?" asked the MD after introducing himself as Hugo Browning.

Masters, sensing the hostility, half wished he had something nasty to parade before the man, just to bring him down to a more co-operative level. But he overcame the temptation to blurt out words like murder which might shock, and instead said, very mildly, "I was wondering if you could put me in touch with somebody who could talk to me about a man called Louis Packard, who was a representative of yours until five or six years ago. Somebody who knew him well."

"Packard, you say! Why, what's he done?"

"As far as we know, at the moment, nothing more heinous than disappear completely. But he has been gone since last November, and with him went an almost new and expensive car together with other valuable bits and pieces, including research results, which the car contained."

"Car been found yet?"

"No hint of the car or the man, and for reasons I won't bore you with, Mr Browning, we regard that as distinctly odd. It is one of the factors which have led us to the conclusion that Packard may no longer be alive, rather than to the more obvious answers such as desertion to another woman or loss of memory."

Browning now appeared to be more intrigued than hostile. He shepherded them to the end of the office opposite to the one occupied by his desk, and invited them to take seats—almost exact replicas of those in Emery's office—around a coffee table.

"It's obvious, Mr Masters, that your best bet would be to meet somebody who was a rep at the same time as Packard and in the same area."

"Which was, I believe, the north-east of Essex and Suffolk."

"Roughly that, I seem to remember. Don't be surprised at my knowledge, young lady," he said to Tip. "I was Sales Director at the time. I've gone up in the world a bit since then, but it doesn't mean I've completely lost my memory."

"I'm sorry if I looked surprised, sir, but I've been looking across at the map on your wall and I see the country is divided into over ninety representative territories. To remember who was where more than five years ago. . . ."

Browning laughed. "You're as observant as you are personable."

"I'm a Detective Sergeant in the senior team at the Yard," said Tip proudly, reddening as she spoke.

"I'm sure you must be a very competent person," replied Browning, "because my memory has stirred again, and I have now remembered that even I have heard and read of the reputation which Mr Masters has earned himself. It makes me wonder why such a man is undertaking an enquiry so. . . ."

"So what, Mr Browning?"

Browning spread his hands. "Your scene is murder,

Mr Masters. I know you said you think Packard is very likely dead, but the case is still merely one of disappearance. Am I not right?"

"Fortunately the number of murders I am called upon to investigate does not fill my time completely," replied Masters drily.

"Amen to that," murmured Browning. "Now where were we? Packard's territory. North-east Essex, including biggish towns like Chelmsford and Colchester and scads of smaller places, some of which, like Witham, were—and are—growing quickly. He made a good job of his patch. A born seller."

"So you were sorry to lose him when he decided to move to Alpurplas."

"Well . . . yes, obviously. In some ways."

"Please tell me the ways you weren't sorry about."

"There was nothing that could have interested the police."

"At that time, probably not. But now. . . . Look, Mr Browning, a psychiatrist has to dig deep into the past to understand today's ills before he can attempt a cure. We're much the same in a case like this. You were not entirely sorry to lose Packard, yet you say he was good at his job, which was, after all, doing your work for you. Had he been a man of pleasant character, you would have been totally sorry to see him go. That means that you discovered in him defects of character of a nature serious enough to balance out his good qualities as a salesman. And defects in character are apt to get the backs of other people well and truly up. Somewhere along the line Packard could have made an enemy who waited until he saw a chance for revenge. Nothing to interest the police, you said. Maybe not, at the time, but if the score has now been settled in such a way that Packard is no longer alive, then it is most definitely not only of interest to me, it is my business and it becomes yours to tell me of it."

"There were no facts."

"I'll listen to rumours. And if it is of any help to you, or if it eases your conscience at all, perhaps I should tell you that yesterday we got a less than flattering report on Packard's character from Alpurplas. The sales director there said that Packard was a hard man and one who would never forgive or forget the slightest word or action he found to be not to his liking. That's merely a summary."

"So I won't be telling tales out of school if I say we found Packard to be much the same?"

"Not at all, but I'm hoping you will amplify that."

"I can—by rumour only, as I suggested."

"I'd like to hear what you have to say."

"It will be a longish story. I'll have some coffee brought in before I start."

After the coffee arrived Browning told his PA to stall any visitors and not to put calls through for the next hour. As Tip started to pour the coffee, the managing director began his story.

"About the time I'm talking of, five or so years ago and only a matter of weeks before Packard resigned from AVL, the financial climate in pharmaceutical firms was somewhat different from that of today. Now we are restricted in so many ways we can hardly keep our heads above water. That is by the by. But in those days we could afford to call all our reps together once a year for an annual conference which we held at some resort abroad. Actually, it probably didn't cost us as much as it would have done to put them into a British hotel, but the field force appreciated it, and it was our best way of thanking them for the work of the previous year.

"That year we went to Germany. Not by plane, as we usually did, but by boat from Harwich. We used a train on the continent, but to get to Harwich the reps used the cars supplied by the firm. But not all the cars were to be brought. The reps were to double up, at least, and most vehicles converged on Harwich with three or even four reps aboard. As you can imagine, there is a long-stay park there to take them.

"Like you, we employ women in our ranks. Women reps, I mean."

"Packard was entangled with one of them?" asked Masters. "And used the conference as an opportunity to further the relationship?"

"He may have had his bit of fun for all I know, but that wasn't what I was going to mention."

"Sorry for the interruption."

"No matter. No, the reason I told you about our girl reps was because one of them had, about a year previously, married one of the male reps. Alan Kempe was also an Eastern Region rep, and lived in Ipswich. His new wife, Annabel, moved from her parents' home somewhere up near Peterborough to live with him, but she kept her former patch, which was, very roughly, the county of Norfolk. I think their idea was eventually to move further north, so that they would be on the doorstep of both territories if she travelled northwards and he southwards.

"That is all just background so that you will understand some of the geography of what came later—on the return from the German conference."

Browning sighed. "I expect, like me, Mr Masters, you find that if some people can add complications to the simplest of arrangements they will do so. In theory we were all to get off the boat at Harwich that Friday, pick up our cars, and disperse to our individual homes throughout the UK. But not a bit of it. Different people wanted to go here, there and everywhere. Not that it bothered me, and I let them get on with it. One lot of those arrangements is, however, pertinent to this story.

"Alan and Annabel Kempe were not the only married couple in the field force. There were, actually, three or four such couples. One pair, Peter and Gwen Harrowby, who lived and worked up on Tyneside—still do if it comes to that—were quite friendly with the Kempes. I mentioned we returned to Harwich on the Friday. It was the early evening boat. We'd been travelling since very early morning, so the prospect of a long drive on this side was not all that inviting.

"Anyhow, rearrangements were made. The Harrowbys

62

shed the two passengers they had picked up in Yorkshire on the way down so that they, the Harrowbys, could stay overnight with the Kempes and then drive north on the Saturday.

"Ipswich is quite close to Harwich, of course, so the Kempes had not had to give anybody a lift to the boat. That meant there were two couples, in two cars, to go to Ipswich.

"The Harrowbys had never been to the Kempes' house, apparently, even though they were friendly within the confines of the field force, and I don't know if you know Ipswich, but for a first time visitor it is a bit difficult to find your way even though it's not all that big a place. The upshot was that Alan Kempe arranged to drive alone in his own car while Annabel joined the Harrowbys to act as guide for them. As he hadn't to wait to show the way, Alan Kempe went off at his own pace, a minute or two before the others left the car park. So he reached home first, quite a time ahead of his wife and guests, actually, because Annabel had to stop and buy milk and bread and what-have-you for the four of them."

Browning stopped at this point and drained the coffee pot into his cup. When he looked up he said to Masters, "What I'm going to tell you now is hearsay from a number of different sources, and probably coloured a bit by my own imagination. But I will try to make it as unembellished as possible."

"Thank you. You have done famously so far."

"This is Kempe's account of the subsequent events. He said he went straight home and, because he knew there would be the Harrowby car to park on the path inside the house gate, he ran his car straight into the garage and closed the doors. Closed, mark you. He said he didn't lock them because he had heard the two wives discussing the possibility of them all going out for dinner that evening and he thought he might need the car again.

"He went in and opened up the house, by which time it was dusk—springtime, you see. Then the second car arrived and pulled into the little drive. After that, apparently, they had a pot of tea and a brush-up and, as he had supposed they would, they went off to some restaurant for an early dinner. They only needed one car for the purpose, so as it was the easy one to get at, they used the one belonging to Harrowby. Kempe says he forgot to lock his garage."

"An easy thing to overlook," acknowledged Masters.

"Quite. But now comes the meat of the story. That same evening, during the time both those cars were driving from Harwich to Ipswich, on a quiet, rural stretch of road, a young girl of fourteen or fifteen was knocked down and killed. The driver didn't stop. Though the exact time of the accident could not be fixed with any certainty, the police forensic people—as you know they can—immediately discovered that the car that had knocked her down had left a scrap or two of red paint on her clothing and that the make-up of those scraps was that used by Ford for painting red Cortinas."

Tip could not hold the question back. "Were the cars supplied by AVL to their reps red Cortinas, sir?"

"At that time, yes. For ordinary reps, identical red Cortinas."

"There must be a twist in the tail of this story," said Masters, "but the obvious outcome would seem to be that the car with the crumpled bumper was discovered in Kempe's garage."

"More or less right."

"But it couldn't have been Kempe," said Tip, "because his wife and the Harrowbys weren't all that far behind him and they would have found the girl."

"Ah!" said Browning, "you've put your finger on something there, young woman. Remember Kempe had lived for some years in Ipswich—long enough to have bought a house and put down roots, and as a consequence, like all reps, he knew the roads in the area very well indeed, even though Harwich was not within his territory. He took a B road, I forget its number, which skirts the south bank of the estuary of the River Stour and turns north through Manningtree before running a few short miles into Ipswich. If you're interested, you'll be able to look that up for yourself. Mrs Kempe, however, was not familiar with the lesser roads in that area. Remember she had lived in Ipswich a comparatively short time and the territory she knew well was forty or fifty miles further north. So when she was acting as guide for the Harrowbys, she used the major road, the A604, I think it is, which joins the main A12(T) just north of Colchester and then runs straight into Ipswich."

"I know that bit, sir. It's the old Roman road, isn't it?"

"I believe it is. So you see Annabel Kempe and the Harrowbys were not on Kempe's tail during the run back to Ipswich, so they could not claim that they had passed along the same route and had seen no accident at that time."

Masters nodded his understanding of that point and then said: "Two things occur to me, Mr Browning."

"Yes?"

"As one of your reps, Mrs Kempe would also have had one of your red Cortinas. From what you have told us so far, it wasn't at the house."

"Quite right. Mrs Kempe had put it into the local garage for a service while she was away. All the cars were nearly new at the time, and we insisted that proper checks and oil changes and so on were carried out at the correct mileages."

"Thank you. I should have guessed that."

Browning shrugged. "You spotted the point. What was the second one you spotted?"

"You stressed that reps get to know the roads in their territories very well indeed. I believe that Harwich and Colchester were in Packard's territory. Are you suggesting that Packard would have used the same minor road out of Harwich as the one Kempe took?"

Browning grimaced. "That is my belief, and that of several of my reps at the time—the local district manager among them. You see, that road, where Kempe turned north at Manningtree, carries straight on towards Colchester. It, too, joins the A12(T), just where it emerges from the by-pass. So all Packard then had to do was to follow the by-pass for the few miles to where it joins the A120."

"At Mark's Tey," said Tip. "It's a Roman road, too. Stane Street."

Browning looked at her admiringly. "If ever the police wish to dispense with your services, Sergeant, apply to me for a job. I could use an encyclopaedic mind like yours. Most of my young women are so forgetful they'd lose their heads if they were loose."

Browning turned to Masters. "That road runs due west through Braintree and Great Dunmow to hit the M11 at Bishop's Stortford. Turn south there, and you are in the area of Theydon Bois in no time at all. And Packard lived in that area. I remember he bought a house there because he said it would be handy for the M25 when it finally came to be built."

"His wife still lives there," said Masters. "Sergeant Tippen and I visited her yesterday afternoon."

"So he still works the same area for Alpurplas, does he?"

"He's the district manager for East Anglia."

"Still his old stamping ground, then."

"Yes. Has that some significance to your mind, Mr Browning?"

"None that I can think of."

"But you were at pains to tell us that he could have followed the same route from Harwich as Kempe did. You must attach some significance to that, otherwise why mention it?"

"I was also at pains to tell you that this latter part of my story is rumour, hearsay or whatever. There is no evidence to support it."

"I'm here to listen. I'll start you off by asking how the local police got on to Kempe. His damaged car was hidden away in the garage."

"Kempe told them himself. He claims to have known nothing about the hit-and-run and so, next morning, when he went into his garage for the car, after the Harrowbys had left, and saw the damage, he immediately rang the police to report what he said he thought had been an act of vandalism by yobbos who had found the garage unlocked while he was out at dinner the evening before."

"The act of an honest citizen, in fact."

"Quite. But as soon as the local police heard of a red Cortina with a crumpled wing and other bits and pieces of damage consistent with having hit a human body, they were on to it like a sparrow on to a crumb. When they then heard that Kempe had driven along the minor road the evening before, more or less at the time the girl had been struck, Kempe had had it."

"Protesting his innocence the whole time?"

"Just so, and being branded a liar by the police. They'd found that plastic corner bit of a front bumper. You know what I mean. It's meant to fall off on impact. It's a wrap round bit that is held on with plastic clips. The police had found it at the scene of the accident, and that piece was missing from Kempe's car."

"A policeman's dream, in fact? An open and shut case?"

Browning nodded. "And Kempe went down for it. Courts don't like drivers who knock kids over, kill them, and drive on without stopping."

"Manslaughter, I suppose?"

"Three years. Shortened a bit, of course."

"He obviously left you at the time, but what about his wife?"

"She left us—of her own free will—after the trial."

"To do what?"

"I don't know. But she didn't give in, of that I'm sure. She was made of pretty stern stuff and, of course, she accepted her husband's word without reservation as, indeed, did all his colleagues who knew him. You see, he was a kindly man. A gentle soul."

"That doesn't sound much like the description of the archetypal rep we've heard about these last few days."

Browning laughed. "It doesn't seem typical, does it? But there are some men who can succeed in the job by force of personality alone. I don't mean overpowering personality. Just decent, probably even mild-mannered, men whom nobody minds seeing again and again because they are such pleasant people to meet at any time. You must have met them. All too infrequently, perhaps. But they do exist. Kempe was one of them. A biggish chap, gentle with a soft voice and a good countenance. I liked him a lot, and so did the doctors on his territory. They made a friend of him—or most of them did—as they got to know him more and more. They called him by his first name, and their staffs almost invariably welcomed him. He helped them in innumerable ways and he had their affection. Nobody who knew him believed he had hit that girl and left her to die."

"Could he have hit her and not known?" asked Tip. "You said it was growing dusk."

"It was by the time he got home," acknowledged Browning, "but if Kempe had hit her he couldn't have failed to know. The damage to the nearside wing and the flasher was far too great not to have been noticed."

"You said 'if' Kempe hit her. The court obviously decided he did," said Masters. "There is a doubt in your mind."

"Yes."

"Yet the mangled car was that driven by Kempe."

"People knocked their heads together over this one," replied Browning. "Annabel was the prime mover. She refused to believe her husband guilty, so if not Alan Kempe, who could it have been? They came to see me, two or three of them together."

"For what purpose?"

"To point out to me that the wings on their Cortinas were easily removable and therefore easily replaceable. About twelve bolts. Fast nuts, spire bolts, fast threads with no nuts and easy to undo, especially on a new car. And the flasher, just held on by a bolt, with a wire to be simply unplugged. Glass held on with two screws only.

There's a wire to go through the bolt before the nut goes back on, but that's the only fiddly bit."

"I'm following, just."

"And I'm talking in shorthand and because I'm no car mechanic and I'm recalling what those people told me all those years ago."

"What was their point?"

"They had tried it. One rep, not a mechanic, had exchanged wings and flashers on two cars in just two hours. He'd then had to make the mastic good and retouch the inside of the engine bay, which took him the best part of another hour. Three hours in all. Packard, they told me—although I knew it for myself—was a skilled amateur mechanic who knew his way about cars and carried a comprehensive tool kit with him."

"Go on."

"They said he had taken the same route as Kempe, but somewhat later because he had stopped for tea in a café before leaving Harwich. Evidently Packard was very fond of tea and sweet gooey cakes. He indulged daily whenever possible."

"Fact?"

"They said they'd established his movements."

"But you didn't yourself check up on it?"

"How could I? I had no authority."

"Your reps? Did they approach the police?"

"Two of them did. The ones who had changed the wings. A police sergeant heard them out and said, 'So what? You can change the wings on a Cortina in two hours. That's not evidence of anything except your ability to change the wings on a Cortina.' And he was right to say that, although I suppose that somebody with a little more imagination might have pursued it further. For instance, I would have thought it would have been possible to test if the bolts had been newly inserted or the mastic was old."

"Are you sure it wasn't done?"

"Of course not."

"So what you are saying is that some of your people

believed that Packard had hit the girl and had then changed wings with Kempe to make it look as though he had killed her."

"That was what they believed."

"There are a number of objections to such a theory."

"Such as?"

"First off, Packard would have needed to know the arrangements the Kempes and Harrowbys had made for the evening."

Browning nodded. "That is a difficult one, I'll admit, but my people said that all these arrangements had been made quite openly and anybody in the field force could have overheard. But I will admit that there was no way Packard could have known he would find a Cortina at Kempe's place. The two couples could well have taken a car each."

Masters smiled. "Even if they had, that wouldn't have worried him."

"Why?"

"Because he'd have expected to find a third one there. That belonging to Mrs Kempe. I don't suppose he knew it had gone in for a service and it would have served his purpose just as well as her husband's."

"By jove, so he would. But he couldn't have known the garage would have been left open for him."

"That was a stroke of luck, admittedly, but I don't suppose the double door of an ordinary house garage would worry a good mechanic all that much. Always supposing, of course, that Packard was involved in a switch."

"There is that proviso," admitted Browning, "but my people were convinced of his complicity. He wasn't exactly liked and admired by his colleagues at any time, and after that the feeling towards him grew pronouncedly anti. He caught a couple of them trying to get a look under his bonnet to see if there were any signs of tampering there. We nearly had a nasty incident because of it. I think the hostility at last got through to Packard and he gave notice of his intention to resign to join Alpurplas. I was sorry to lose a good rep and happy to see the back of Packard, if you understand what that implies."

"I think I do."

"When he handed his car in, I had a mechanic at our main fleet garage here go over it. Of course, I couldn't say too much about what I wanted him to look for, and the report came back that it was the best maintained rep's car the chap had ever seen. Everything in the engine bay was clean, polished, greased, oiled, touched-up and so on. Like a new car only better, the mechanic said."

"And that was the last you heard of Packard?"

"Yes. I was glad when the whole business was over. Of course, we couldn't keep Kempe, though I tried to persuade Annabel to stay on. Somewhere at the back of my mind I had the idea that when he came out of prison I would move them both to adjoining territories as far away as possible from East Anglia. But, as I said, Annabel decided to leave us. We did what we could for Kempe. All the time he was inside we sent him everything he was allowed to have, and his colleagues stood by him pretty well. Those closest to him visited when it was convenient for Annabel to let them do so."

"I see. Well, Mr Browning, you've given me a lot to think about. Thank you both for the information and for your time." He got to his feet. "There's a sad side to all this, you know."

"Is there? What's that?"

"I shall be obliged to seek out the Kempes and speak to them."

"No, no! Please. You asked me to illustrate Packard's character for you. I would never have told you this story had I thought I would be stirring up trouble and embarrassment for two perfectly decent people who, in my opinion, have been given more than their fair share of ill-treatment already."

"I don't think a visit from me can be regarded as ill-treatment, Mr Browning."

"Oh, yes it can. Most of us like and respect our police

as long as they stay in their stations or on the streets. We do not welcome you coming to our homes, particularly gentlemen of your calibre, and especially not if we have been on the receiving end of your activities, whether the treatment has been just or unjust."

"I'm a great believer in fair treatment, Mr Browning, even if it is so belated as not to put right what may have been wrong in the first place. But I also believe in doing my job. Unobtrusively, if possible. Had you not told me what you have told me, I believe I should have ferreted out substantially the same story elsewhere, but perhaps not in a form quite so favourable to Alan Kempe."

"I see."

"Can I ask you not to warn Kempe that I might be paying him a visit? And not to ask anybody else to warn him, either?"

"I'm not sure I can give you that promise."

"Thank you for your honesty. I shall take it then that when I arrive, Kempe will have been warned of my coming. That being the case, I feel sure you will have no objections to giving me his address. It will save asking questions in Ipswich and so, I think, save him from some possible embarrassment."

"Did you ever think of entering the Diplomatic Service, Mr Masters?"

"I'm in one of them already."

"The devil you are. I'll get you that address. And I promise I will not warn Kempe."

"Or Mrs Kempe, please."

"Or Mrs Kempe," agreed Browning.

As soon as they were in the car, Masters consulted the road atlas to get the lay-out of the routes from Harwich to Ipswich clear in his mind.

"B 1352 to Manningtree. Turn north near the railway station for Cattawade and Brantham and then almost immediately turn left and it's only a drive and a chip into Ipswich. But it is only a broad between Harwich and Manningtree, so it must have been along that stretch that the girl was killed. Whoever knocked her down, Kempe or Packard, would therefore have to pass through Manningtree and the other villages, to say nothing of however much of Ipswich had to be negotiated to get to Kempe's house."

"You're thinking of the crumpled wing, sir?"

"Yes. What do you think about it?"

"If Kempe had knocked her down, he would have been driving in broad daylight in a badly damaged car. The dusk only came down as he reached home. Easy for somebody to see the damage, which would be dangerous for him. By the same token, Chief, you might say he had a good reason for putting the car in the garage, out of sight of the others when they arrived."

"Go on."

"Packard, who must have been quite a time behind Kempe, would probably be arriving at Manningtree just as darkness fell, so he wouldn't be so easily seen, but against that he'd be driving in the dark without a near-side flasher. So I think the odds are about even."

"You think Packard without a nearside flasher would be more noticeable than Kempe with a crumpled wing?"

"Yes, sir, I do."

"Not so, Tip."

"Why not, sir?"

"You have to use your flashers even in daylight."

"I know that, sir."

"Drive along a fairly deserted road at dusk. Put a flasher on to turn left. The important people to warn, those behind you, see your rear signal. You don't inconvenience oncoming traffic by turning left without showing a front flasher. And if you want to turn right—well, you've got both front and rear lights working normally. I think Packard would get away without being noticed as having a battered wing."

"So you think Packard is the likely one."

"I do, Tip, for one other very good reason."

"Something I've missed, sir."

"Yes. You touched on it and, in my opinion, drew the

wrong conclusion. You suggested Kempe put his car in the garage to shield it from being seen by the others. But, remember, he didn't lock the garage after him. A guilty man would have made sure he had made all safe. He would have locked the garage door."

Tip said nothing for a moment or two, and then: "Sir?"

"Yes, Tip?"

"I made two mistakes out of two, didn't I?"

"You did."

"Not very good for somebody who is sort of on probation is it?"

"No. If you're making similar errors a few weeks from now I shall have to dispense with your services. Reluctantly, from the personal point of view. But I didn't overlook the fact that you drew a commendation from Browning for your grasp of a number of facts this morning. So cheer up. The good points will begin to outweigh the bad when you've been with us a little longer. I don't expect new sergeants to be up to the standard of Berger. I expect to have to train them. Not formally. You've got to learn; to be receptive enough for things to rub off the rest of us and be absorbed by you."

"I understand, sir."

"I'm sure you do. Now stop glooming and get us safely back to the Yard."

"You got my message, Chief?" asked Berger when Masters met Green and the DS on the way to his office.

"I'm sorry, I didn't. I was held up much longer than I expected to be at AVL. Come in and tell me all about it."

As they all sat down, Masters picked up the phoned memo sheet from his blotter. "Here's the route you sent in," he said to Berger. "Grays, Basildon and Southend, staying overnight in Chelmsford. That was on the Monday."

"Yes, Chief, but it's not certain he went that way. He filed that as his route, but the girl in the sales office, who deals with all that sort of admin lark, said Packard swanned about as the fancy took him. The rep for that area lives in Romford and gets around a lot of industrial areas like Dagenham and Canvey Island, so it could be they met that day, but so far we haven't been able to contact the chap. Nor will we be able to until tonight when he gets home. And it's the same with all the other territories."

"Couldn't manage anything better," grunted Green. "The next chap—the one further north—takes in Harlow, Stortford, Braintree, Colchester, Clacton and all places in between. You'd be surprised how many customers there are in small places. Little specialist shops and factories. Trying to trace Packard by applying to men who have to jig about like those reps is no earthly, George. Not after all these months, anyhow."

"Chief," said Tip.

Masters looked up in surprise.

"Yes?"

"When I worked as a typist—before I joined the force, I mean—we had some reps." Tip reddened under the interested gaze of the other three, but ploughed on. "We used to issue diaries for reps to use as day books. Big A5 ones, which our printing department used to make themselves and put together in one of those little binding presses. . . ."

"Go on, love," urged Green.

"It's just that our reps used to like to keep a note of the customers they'd seen and when, and all sorts of bits of information for making up expense sheets, and questions they had to remember to ask when they rang in."

"What you're actually saying, petal," grunted Green, "is that it would be an odd rep who didn't keep some sort of diary."

"Yes."

"But your old firm provided them, and even if Alpurplas doesn't, their travellers will provide themselves with some sort of day book that suits the purpose?"

"I think so. Mr Emery said that all the Alpurplas people are expert salesmen he's poached from other firms.

If they're all that expert they'll be very careful. . . ."

"Meticulous," murmured Masters.

"That's the word, Chief. Meticulous in keeping records, and as they've all come from other firms they'll have brought the habits of other firms with them. Habits like keeping day books."

"Excellent, petal," said Green.

Masters nodded. "If we could get hold of those from the four or five reps in Packard's district. . . ."

"Last year's, Chief," said Tip. "Packard disappeared in November."

"Just so. So we should not be upsetting the commercial life of Alpurplas by asking for them."

"If they've still got them," said Green.

"They have to keep them," said Tip. "They sort of . . . overlap, if you know what I mean. Some calls are probably only made once a year."

Green looked up. "By comparing them we ought to be able to get a pattern of Packard's movements among his troops, George. To help with this 'spot the difference' game I've been hearing about."

"We've certainly got to spot something if the case is not to be bogged down."

"Why? Are we losing momentum?"

"Not as yet. But the way ahead could be a little obscure."

"In what way, Chief?" asked Berger.

"I'll tell you later. First, I want you to listen to Tip, who is going to report on what the two of us heard at AVL this morning."

"From me, Chief?"

"Certainly. Go ahead."

"Let's have it all, flower," said Green, lighting a cigarette. "Take your time, and don't say 'you know' at the end of every other sentence."

"I'll try not to." Tip moistened her lips, nervously, glanced at Masters, who studiously refused to return the gaze and busied himself with packing a pipe, and then began.

"The Chief and I visited the main office of Ayre Valley Laboratories this morning. They usually refer to themselves as AVL. Specifically, we met and talked with Mr Hugo Browning, who is the current managing director but who was sales director at the time Packard was employed there."

"Hang on a moment, sugar," said Green. "Could you make it a bit more matey? Let down a bit, there's a love, and then we'll be interested. At the moment you sound like somebody reading out a chunk from the instructions for filling in income tax forms."

"Sorry . . . er . . . Mr Hugo Browning, too plump, too well dressed, wearing enough perfume to make a Roman Catholic thurible going full blast smell like a barn just evacuated by pigs, and wearing enough gold about his person to suggest he would enjoy the experience of being mugged twice a day."

"Good," said Green drily. "Now we have a lovely picture of him. Could he talk as well?"

"And how! First off he was nervous at the Chief being there, and then when he got the reason for our visit he really opened up."

Masters lit his pipe gravely. Bill Green was giving the girl a lesson in how to report, but Tip was giving as good as she got. He felt pleased about it. One of his fears about her appointment was that she might be overwhelmed by being the lone woman in the team. Now he felt he need no longer worry on that score. Nor, apparently, on her ability to recall this morning's conversation. She was doing better than he had dared hope. Just one or two little things were slipping through the net, but it was a fair enough exposition. He sat back and listened closely. Now the girl was well into her stride she appeared to have forgotten his presence.

She came to the end of her account.

"Excellent," said Masters. "You missed one or two small points. The fact that Packard stopped for tea. . . ."

"Oh, yes. Sorry. He always had tea. Every day. Sticky buns and cream cakes. We might be able to find out where he stopped off to enjoy them and fill out his itinerary that way."

"Good thinking, lass."

"You also forgot to pass on that the feeling against Packard within the AVL field force after Kempe's conviction grew so great that Browning supposed it to be a major contributory factor in Packard's resignation. That could be an important point, because it is at odds with what Emery told us yesterday about poaching Packard from AVL, luring him with the promise of more money."

"Why so important, Chief?" asked Berger.

"Because, lad," said Green, not waiting for Masters to reply, "getting out of AVL like that, so quickly, could show a guilty conscience. If Packard had not been involved with the girl's death, wouldn't he have been siding with his mates in trying to prove Kempe's innocence? And, being the hard case he was supposed to have been, wouldn't he have told a few people where to go and what to do with themselves if he had got a hint that they suspected him and he was clean?"

"That's roughly what I was thinking of," said Masters. "All our information so far points to Packard having been very good, if not outstanding, at his job. Being the man he was, he would know that. Would know his worth to AVL, in fact. If somebody, like Emery, came along and offered him another five hundred a year to join Alpurplas, don't you think he would have filed up to Browning to try to get an extra five hundred out of him before resigning?"

"If he was not guilty, you mean?"

"Yes. I feel certain that such must be the normal reaction of a man who knows for sure that he is recognized by his bosses as being an outstanding employee." He turned to Tip. "What do you say, having been in a commercial front-office at one time?"

"I would bet on your being right, Chief."

"Thank you. Would you also say that a man guilty of a crime and known to be so by his colleagues would leave without chancing his arm over pay?"

"Definitely, Chief. If an employee is not one the boss is keen to keep, he will regard a 'pay-me-more-or-I-resign' move as blackmail, and accept the resignation without any hesitation at all."

"Yet Packard, knowing his worth, did not make that move."

"QED," said Green airily.

"So where are we, Chief?" asked Berger.

"At the point where I said I would tell you later about our momentum. Packard is missing, we don't know where. We assume he is dead, but we have no solid proof. We believe him to be guilty of a crime five or six years ago for which another man paid the penalty. This last based on circumstantial evidence, rumour, and hearsay, which in turn has sprung almost entirely from his knowledge of a certain stretch of B road and his acknowledged ability as a car mechanic."

"Nothing there," said Green. "Unless we're going to assume that this gentle-mannered giant, Kempe, has lain in wait for five or six years to take his revenge. But that really won't do, will it? Kempe might have suspected Packard of framing him, but he had no proof, otherwise it would have been brought up in court. And it wasn't. Kempe went down and Packard remained at large. So what's to do? Without knowing what has happened to Packard, we can't go calling on Kempe and asking if he's seen his old enemy lately and if so, has he knocked him on the head and buried the body."

"I see what you mean," murmured Berger, "and what you meant, Chief, when you suggested we might be bogged down. But what about your 'spot the difference' game? We reckon we've spotted one discrepancy. That doesn't prove Packard killed the young girl, but it has helped to bolster his guilt in our minds."

Masters leaned back in his chair. "Nobody has yet mentioned the biggest discrepancy of all between the Alpurplas and AVL report on Packard."

"What's that, Chief?" asked Tip.

"A clean slate from one and not from the other."

"And the leopard doesn't change its spots," grunted Green. "A dirty great blot on one little picture and not on the other. Either AVL are entirely wrong about Packard or Alpurplas have not yet found him out. Or if they have, they're saying nothing about it."

"More villainy?" asked Berger.

"What do you think, lad?"

"It hurts me to say it, but I think you could be right. AVL ran a tight shop. No overnight stays anywhere except at home for their reps. Drug samples, unless they're narcotics, are not worth flogging, and AVL doesn't make narcotics. It makes nice little ointments and suppositories. . . ."

"Don't stop, lad."

"His skullduggery came out in another way while he was with AVL. Now, with Alpurplas it probably comes out in financial fiddles. . . ."

"See bundles of bank notes," murmured Tip.

". . . which they either don't know about or ignore because of his undoubted value to the firm." Berger stopped suddenly, snapped his fingers, and turned to Green. "What were Emery's exact words when he said he had mentioned the prospect of promotion to Packard?"

Green sat up. "Wait a moment. Emery said he told Packard he would get the job of district manager 'as long as he continued the good work and kept his nose clean.' That was it, exactly. And then he went on to say Packard was a nice chap if he wasn't crossed." He turned to Masters. "The second of those two statements must have been based on experience. Friend Louis must have had a run-in with somebody at Alpurplas —probably more than one—for Emery to be so sure of his character. I mean the suggestion that in order to repay a grudge he might put arsenic in your beer when you weren't looking was probably going a bit far, but you must admit it's a pretty strong pointer as to

80

Packard's type. And as for telling a man considered fit to take over a senior management post that he'll get the job if he keeps his nose clean . . . well, an executive just doesn't say that sort of thing to a mature man of proven ability in the job unless there have been occasions when that man has not always been above a bit of skullduggery."

Masters considered this for a moment or two and then said: "It sounds feasible. Thanks, the two of you, for bringing that up. We should be able to make something of your conclusions." He turned to Tip. "You see how unguarded remarks from people you interview can help and so must be remembered very carefully?"

"I hoisted that inboard, Chief."

"Now she's getting sassy," groaned Green.

"Finding her feet," remonstrated Berger.

Masters smiled. "Joining the team," he said. "You can't expect a newcomer to learn some of our ways and not others."

"The trouble with all youngsters," said Green, "is that they pick up your bad habits quicker than your good ones." He grinned at the girl. "And if you say we've got a hell of a lot of bad ones to copy you'll be buying my beer for a fortnight."

"I'll take out a mortgage for it," replied Tip.

Masters got to his feet. "We'll break for lunch. This afternoon, Bill, I'd like you to return to Alpurplas and get Emery to tell you if you're right about what his comments implied."

"To get the blot on both little pictures?"

"To see if there should be one on both."

"Will do."

"Take Tip with you. The two of you can continue her education. I've got a bit of work I want to do here."

"Anything we should know about?"

"Phone calls. To the locals in all the places on the routes you brought in. I thought a personal word might just bring something to light about the car. I shall also ask them to keep their eyes open and to call us should anything crop up about anything which might interest us."

"Good idea," said Green. "Old boy basis. Works wonders sometimes."

4

Masters felt he had to get out and about if he were really to grapple with the problem of Packard's disappearance. So far he had no indication of where the man had been last seen or even where to centre himself and the team to start looking for him. But he had made up his mind that if Kempe still lived in Ipswich, that is where he would go, if only because he wished to interview Kempe.

His first call was Bury St Edmunds. Might he approach Ipswich with a problem? Permission given. Wait ten minutes to allow Bury to talk to Ipswich and tell them the Yard wanted some help. Meanwhile, talk to Colchester to ask to be informed if a man answering to Packard's description had ever come to their attention, alive or dead. The same for the car. No? If they heard or saw anything would they please let him, Masters, know immediately.

For George Masters, anything. The local bobbies would be instructed to be extra vigilant.

Back to Ipswich.

"This is Detective Chief Superintendent Masters of Scotland Yard. If he is available I should like to speak to your DCI."

"DCI Knight."

"Good afternoon, Mr Knight. DCS Masters of Scotland Yard here. I was wondering. . . ."

"DCS *George* Masters?"

"Yes. I've been to Bury St Edmunds to ask if I could seek your help."

"Yes, Mr Masters. And Bury have been on to me, but

they didn't tell me that it was you who had asked for help."

"Does it make a difference?"

"In theory, no, Mr Masters. But in practice, yes. I mean, to blokes like me in CID, your reputation is a sort of mountain peak we'd all like to climb."

"You flatter me, Mr. Knight. We in the Met get the bigger opportunities to show off."

"There's that, no doubt, sir. But it's still nice to hear we might be able to do something for you."

"Thank you. The case I'm on is a pretty nebulous one."

"Most of them are, aren't they?"

"I think there's some truth in that, but this time we've not so far discovered a body."

"Crikey. You mean somebody has disappeared who you reckon has been murdered?"

"That more or less sums it up, Mr Knight. The whole business started in the Met area, but as so often happens it appears it could have spilled over into other areas."

"Meaning ours, here, in Ipswich and round about?"

"I can't be absolutely sure of that, but perhaps you can help me. While we've been asking questions, the name of a man who used to live in Ipswich cropped up. His name is Kempe, spelt with a final E. Now about six years ago, he was convicted on a hit-and-run charge."

"In our area?"

"Near you somewhere. Did he go through your hands? He killed a schoolgirl while he was driving back from Harwich."

"If we'd dealt with him on a charge like that, I'm sure I'd have remembered. On his way back from Harwich, you say?"

"Yes. He took the B1352 as far as Manningtree and . . ."

"Ah, that's south of the River Stour, Mr Masters. In Essex. Not our area if the hit-and-run happened there."

"I see."

"I tell you what, I could ring Colchester and ask, if you like."

"If you wouldn't mind doing that just to get Kempe's address at the time and then checking up to see whether he still lives in your area, I should be most grateful."

"Give me half an hour, Mr Masters. Was there anything else?"

"It will depend on whether Kempe is still with you. If he's debunked, I shall have to get on to him elsewhere."

"Right. You'll be in your office?"

"All afternoon."

"Not you again, Mr Green," said Cecil Emery, sales director of Alpurplas. "And with reinforcements, too," he added, looking at Tip with appreciation despite the resignation of his tone.

"Me again," agreed Green.

"What is it this time?"

Green opened his eyes wide. "Surely you expected a few supplementaries after we'd had time to digest what you told us the first time—or didn't tell us, as the case may be?"

"I don't think I like the sound of that," said Emery with a frown. "I told you everything . . ."

"That you thought politic," Green ended for him. "Can we sit down?"

"What? Oh, yes. But this politic business. What do you mean by that?"

Green lowered himself into one of the armless easy chairs, and waited till the others were settled before looking across at Emery. Then he said: "When we're just talking to people, like yourself, as opposed to questioning suspects and the like, we usually get what appears to be a very full story, on the face of it. People are co-operative. They say a lot which is often very helpful. But long years of experience have taught us that very few people ever give us a complete picture. Most keep something back. Something they'd rather we didn't know. Not because we might consider it criminal, but because—for reasons best known to themselves—they would rather we didn't know it."

"And you think I've done that?"

"I won't answer your question direct," said Green. "At least not until I've finished what I was saying. Which is this. After talking to somebody who can give us information, we go back to the Yard and chew over everything that has been said. That's what gives rise to supplementaries, and why we have to come back, like we are doing now. You see, Mr Emery, every long conversation, when taken bit from bit, yields clues as to what's not been said. What the talker wants to hide, if you like. It's often as informative to us as what has actually been brought out into the open."

"I repeat my question. You think I held back on Louis Packard?"

"You didn't tell us what fiddles or other misdemeanours you suspected him of—may even have caught him at."

"That is an outrageous statement."

"Not it," grunted Green, taking out his cigarettes. He turned to Berger. "Tell him, lad, while I light up."

"You told us, Mr Emery, that Packard was a hard man and one who would settle scores, however slight, with added interest. You also stressed that he was a first-class salesman whom you had poached from his former employers because of his ability in the field, and then went on to say that because of his outstanding record you were soon to promote him to what is, I imagine, a very senior position."

"Very senior indeed."

"You also said that you treated your sales people very well financially and that you rewarded excellence most liberally."

"Very highly, certainly."

"Well, sir, we have reason to believe that Packard was a man who looked after number one, even at the expense of the company in which he worked. In other words, he did business on the side, indulged in financial fiddles and so on."

"What do you expect me to say to that?"

"We expect you to tell us what his little games were, and explain why you didn't tell us about them at our first meeting."

"I don't think I need to reply to either half of your expectation."

"But you must, mustn't you?" asked Tip, innocently. "If you refuse to answer you as good as confirm that Packard was not playing straight with you. He didn't play straight with AVL, you know, and the leopard doesn't change its spots."

"Don't quote clichés at me, young lady."

"Very good, sir," replied Tip. "So tell us what he did. Did he buy hotel bills? Work the petrol game?"

"You have no right to ask me to incriminate a man for crimes about which I have no proof. I think perhaps I should call our legal director."

"Do that," encouraged Green. "Like us he'll probably want to know why you said to a man whom you were about to promote to a senior position in the company that he would get the job if he kept up the good work, but kept his nose clean, too."

"That was just a figure of speech."

"Something like the cliché you objected to when Sergeant Tippen used it?"

"Yes, I suppose so."

"Nonsense, Mr Emery. It is not the sort of language a man such as yourself would use to a colleague whom you respected enough to promote in this company at the moment of announcing his advancement to him. That remark was a warning. Against what? I think not only your legal director but your financial director also might like to know the answer to that. They might wonder whether your liberal rewards for excellence in the field did not include turning a blind eye on various little habits of Packard's which were, to put it bluntly, robbing the firm rotten. They might ask why, too. And then it would come to light that you would accept anything that would send your sales figures soaring."

87

"Rubbish," said Emery. "A few hundreds a year wouldn't . . ."

"Just a few hundreds?"

"Yes. Which I would have given him in salary and bonuses if he hadn't taken it the way he did. But he was like an incurable gambler. He was only happy if he thought he could outsmart me to get his extra cash. I recognized that pretty quickly, so I let him play along so long as it kept him happy and he continued his good work. Why not? We weren't losing anything by it."

"But he was getting away with it tax free, wasn't he?"

"Not entirely. I suspect those hotel bills Sergeant Tippen mentioned him as buying cost him a fiver a time."

"For a return of what?" asked Tip. "Thirty or thirty-five pounds a time? Dinner, bed and breakfast in good pubs come expensive these days."

Emery shrugged his shoulders. "It was what we would have had to pay had he actually stayed in the hotels, so we lost nothing."

"But he made twenty-five pounds four nights a week? A hundred on that alone each week. What else? Petrol?"

"A good many of them do that," admitted Emery.

"How does it work?" asked Green.

"Go into a garage where you are known, get four gallons put in the tank, pay for five, and get a bill for eight. The garage man is happy to get a couple of extra quid for writing out a bogus bill, while the rep gets sixteen quid out of us for an outlay of ten."

"Fill up every day?" asked Berger. "There's no checking on how much petrol would be used out in the wilds of East Anglia. That must have netted him another twenty-five or thirty a week."

"Hold it," growled Green. "That means he was fiddling six or seven thousand a year, and you said a few hundreds."

"I was right," said Emery. "We would have paid his hotel bills anyway, so that fiddle cost my budget nothing. The petrol . . . four time a week . . . yes, the best part of a thousand a year."

"Just as a matter of interest, where did he stay on the nights when he was supposed to be in the hotels he charged you for?"

"I honestly don't know, but I suspect he had various ports of call. Convenient houses, if you like."

"Convenient houses? You mean people put him up? Women?"

"I've long suspected he knew one or two women who . . . er . . . accommodated him. I've wondered whether they could have been the wives of reps of other companies, perhaps. Childless ones whose husbands were away from home during the working week."

"Any evidence?"

"No direct evidence."

"Indirect then?"

"As I said, suspicions only."

"What aroused your suspicions?"

Emery grimaced. "Packard used to hold selling meetings. They were arranged very carefully. If we were introducing a new product he would invite good customers; if he was just pushing an older product, to give it a boost, he would invite people to whom the product might be useful but who were as yet non-buyers. He'd hold the meeting in a local hotel where he could give these people lunch or dinner, according to the time of day, and at the same time he'd put on a display, give a short talk, or even show a film of the product in use."

"Successful, was it?"

"Very. He was good. Anyhow, one day I paid one of my irregular, unannounced visits to his district. As usual he joined me for dinner in the hotel where he booked me in for the night. I assumed he'd have booked himself in, too. But that's by the way. After dinner—when Packard had left me to go to the gents—the manager came and asked me if I was a colleague of his. When I said I was he said he could offer me the same deal as he had with Packard. I asked for details. In short it was for extra meals to be charged for on the bill at each selling meeting, which would entitle me within reason to unlimited free dinners any night I fancied, or with whom I might fancy."

Green grunted to show he understood. "So what happened?"

"I did nothing immediately and kept my mouth shut. But when Packard announced he wasn't staying at the same hotel and it was time for him to be going, I decided to follow him in the car to see what he was up to. He led me to a biggish cottage. I didn't see anything more except that he went in."

"A convenient house, as you called it?"

"I assumed so. I guessed at some woman there who was providing him with all the comforts while he was away from home."

"Did you tackle him with it later?"

"Next morning. He grew very cagey when I mentioned it. That surprised me because I expected him to tell me it was none of my business in whose bed he spent the night."

"As it wasn't," said Tip.

"Quite. But even so his reaction made me a bit suspicious. What of, I can't say, but I formed the impression there was a bit more to it than just having another woman on the side. I thought it through, and decided there were probably two or three of the convenient houses, scattered about his district."

"He was on to a good thing," said Berger. "Cheap or even free entertainment which you paid him to enjoy and free dinner for himself and his companions of choice. Not bad. I take it his wife did not know about it!"

"I'm sure she didn't. I reckoned that was one of the reasons Packard didn't tell me to mind my own business. He didn't want me to tell Ida."

"Which you didn't?"

"Of course not. Remember I told you he'd get his own back. He'd have got it back on me, somehow."

"How? Had he got anything on you?"

"Nothing."

"Sure?"

"Absolutely sure. But I always felt he would find some way of playing the dirty on me if I had let the cat out of the bag. At the very least he would have resigned, and I didn't want that."

"You've told us everything now, have you?" asked Green.

"Yes."

"Not quite," said Berger. "I'd like to know where that cottage was. The one you followed him to."

"Oh, come on. It was over two years ago. You're not going to start up trouble for whoever she was who lived there—may still live there for all I know—and for Ida Packard?"

"We shan't start any unnecessary trouble, sir," replied Berger, "but I'd still like the address. It may come in useful. If not, we'll forget it."

"It was night time when I followed him."

"Even so, sir."

"Oh very well. It was on a B road, about a mile or so north of a place called Debenham. The cottage was called Walesby, if I remember correctly. It's about a hundred yards south of a track junction where I turned the car."

"Thank you, sir."

"See what I mean about supplementaries, Mr Emery?" asked Green.

"No, I don't. I've told you little or nothing more than you already knew. You knew he was a fiddler so I've only confirmed that, and you could have guessed he might have women friends. Even I'm guessing about that. And as for the name and location of a cottage he visited years ago . . . well, if you call all that further information, good luck to you."

"Thanks."

"I can't for the life of me see how any of it will help you find him, alive or dead."

"Nor can we, yet," agreed Green. "But you never can tell with bees."

"What?"

"You didn't read the proper books when you were a kiddy, Mr Emery, or you wouldn't ask."

"Oh, I see."

Berger opened the office door. "Be seeing you," said Green as he passed through it after Tip.

"I hope not," replied Emery fervently.

Masters lifted the phone when it rang and gave his name.

"DCI Knight here, sir. From Ipswich."

"Yes, Mr Knight. Have you some information for me?"

"I have, Mr Masters. Kempe still lives here, in the same house."

"With Mrs Kempe?"

"Yes, sir. There are no children."

"Have you found out what they're doing?"

"I have, sir. They're running a restaurant."

"Restaurant, did you say?"

"Yes, sir. Quite a well thought of establishment, actually. Open all day from quite early in the morning until fairly late on. Good class. The sort of place where businessmen can have lunch when they're not partial to a boozer, and where middle-aged women go for morning coffee and afternoon tea. I remember I had a sort of late breakfast there once when I'd been up and about all night. I didn't know anything about the owners then, of course. It's called The Capercaillie."

"How much do you know about them now?"

"Nothing concrete, actually, sir. Just the whisper that Kempe found he couldn't get a job when he came out of jail, so he and his wife decided to set up on their own. One of my older sergeants here hired them to cater for his daughter's wedding a bit ago. He was very pleased with them. Good stuff, reasonable price and left his house spotless when they left."

"Thank you, Mr Knight. I may have to come and see Kempe. If I do, I shall call on you if I may."

"It'll be a pleasure, sir. Oh, and if you were thinking of staying. . . ."

"A possibility, perhaps."

"Book in at The Blenheim, sir. It's good. You won't find a better place to stay anywhere. I'll give you the number if you like."

"Thank you. I'll make a note of it now if you've got it handy."

"It's in the useful numbers bit, sir." Knight read it out and advised Masters to book as far in advance as possible.

Masters listened to the account given by Green of the interview with Emery and at the end of it said nothing for so long that Green asked: "What's wrong with you? Cat got your tongue?"

Masters came to with a start. "Sorry, Bill. Thinking about what you've just told me."

"Useful, was it? No, don't answer that. If it's started you thinking that deeply, we've uncovered something pretty valuable. I know that from experience of working with you these last umpteen years. What was it?"

Masters turned to Tip. "You were the one who asked Emery whether Packard was buying hotel bills and playing the petrol game. How did you know about such things?"

Tip reddened. "As you know, Chief, I used to work in the office of a firm that had reps out in the field."

"Before you joined the force? Yes, you told us."

"When it became obvious yesterday afternoon—after we'd seen Mrs Packard and heard the report of the DCI's first interview with Mr Emery—that Louis Packard was pulling some field force fiddles, I rang up a friend I used to work with. He's the under-manager of the department in head office that services the field force. He used to be a rep but his health packed it in. He's not fit at all, really, so they brought him inside to fill a vacancy they had there. He made a good job of it right from the start, because he knows all the wrinkles. No rep pulls the wool over his eyes, Chief."

"Why did you ring him up?"

"To ask him what were the commonest fiddles that reps got up to. He said most reps were pretty honest characters—as much as anybody is honest these days, and he didn't like my asking the question. But I pressed him a bit and he told me about those two because they are more or less common to all field forces where there are rotten apples. However, he did say that a lot of dodges are peculiar to the type of goods and type of selling involved. What he said was, more or less, that there are always opportunities for skullduggery if villains look for them."

"Thank you. That was very good thinking on your part. What do you think, Bill?"

"I think you asked the lass the question in order to duck the one I put to you about what it was in my report that set you thinking so deeply."

"It was the mention of the cottage."

"Walesby Cottage, north of Debenham?"

"Yes. Are you sure Emery said Debenham and not Dereham? I only ask because Debenham sounds like a department store to me, whereas I do know there's a Dereham—East Dereham, in fact—bang slap in the middle of Norfolk."

"He said Debenham," asserted Green.

"Good."

"Why good?"

"Because Dereham is quite a long way from Ipswich." He turned to Berger. "Get the road atlas off the shelf and look it up, please."

Green wasn't to be put off. "Does Kempe still live in Ipswich?"

"Yes. He keeps a restaurant there." Masters then gave a brief account of his phone calls during the afternoon. At the end of it, he said to Green: "You can guess why I'm hoping Berger is going to tell us Debenham is a lot nearer to Ipswich than Dereham."

Green nodded. Berger said: "It is a lot nearer, Chief. As the crow flies it's no more than thirteen or fourteen miles north of Ipswich."

"Thank you. I think that settles it. We'll get over to Ipswich tomorrow, Bill. Meanwhile there are a couple of jobs I'd like the sergeants to do. Berger, you arrange for us to stay at The Blenheim Hotel tomorrow night. And remember it's not the usual booking. You'll need four singles and no twin room such as you and Reed used to share."

Green coughed. "George!"

"Yes, Bill?"

"I think I'd better share with the lad. On economy grounds. Otherwise some bright 'Erb is going to start asking questions and I'd rather they didn't begin to get the idea it would be cheaper to do without me."

"Nonsense, Bill. If our lords and masters wish to put one girl into what has previously been an all-male team, they must expect to make proper provision for her and to pay for it. Your rank entitles you to a room on your own, just as mine does, and so, whenever possible, you will continue to enjoy the privileges of your rank."

"That's right, Chief," agreed Berger. "Let me be the one to suffer."

"Suffer? By getting a single room?" He paused a moment and then said: "Point taken, Sergeant, but don't go on to voice the cause of your suffering."

"Sorry, Chief."

"No harm done. Tip, your job is to do a bit of fast telephoning to find out who owns that cottage. The owner's name will be registered with the appropriate local authority. Which it is, I don't know. Find out, and don't tell them you are from the Yard. Just say you want to approach the owner with a view to making an offer to purchase, and only say that if they demand a reason for asking."

"Right, Chief."

"Off you go then. Local government offices don't stay open all night you know."

Both sergeants left them after Masters had given Berger the number of The Blenheim Hotel. Green immediately turned to Masters. "Come on, George. Out with it. You've got some bright idea."

"I admit I have," grinned Masters, "but it depends entirely on what Tip finds out. Look, Bill, I'd rather you didn't press me just now, because it's after five o'clock and I want to get home early if I can. But if you'll go off as well, pick up Doris and come round for supper and I'll discuss it with you then. In full. Promise."

"Will Wanda mind?"

"Not at all. I'll give her a ring now."

After Wanda had professed herself as delighted at the prospect of having Bill and Doris as guests for the evening, Green left the office. Five minutes later Berger looked in to say he had made the bookings at The Blenheim.

"Thank you."

"And you can tell the DCI not to worry, Chief. About the cost, I mean. It seems that in high summer the hotel has bargain prices. The manager told me that, in Ipswich, hotels are far busier throughout the rest of the year than they are in the holiday season. So they lower room prices a bit to attract custom."

"That sounds reasonable, seeing that Ipswich could hardly be called a holiday resort. Thank you, Sergeant. And by the way, make sure Tip knows she is to appear tomorrow with her gear packed ready for staying away for a few days."

"I've told her that, Chief, and warned her to keep a bag ready packed at all times in her locker. She said she'd have to go into a late-night Markies to pick up a few extra bits of underwear."

"Don't feel too sorry about it, Sergeant. These girls can easily wash out bits and pieces in the handbasins in their rooms and the garments dry overnight."

"Nylons and . . . er . . . things, you mean, Chief."

"Exactly. And by the way, Sergeant. I'm sure Tip can take care of herself, but I want the three of us at all times to treat her with the greatest care. I'm not saying we're to treat her with kid gloves and not to pull her leg, but basically she's got to be able to trust and rely on us implicitly. That's why I suggested you didn't finish the little funny you were going to make about sergeants always sharing twin rooms. I don't want her to feel under any hint of a threat, verbal or otherwise, while she is with us."

"I'll watch it, Chief. I wasn't out to embarrass her."

"I'm very sure of that. I'd trust you with her, you know that. All I'm pointing out is that we used to be four men together. Now we're not. And although we were rarely, if ever, guilty of using even *double entendre* among ourselves, we now have to guard what we say a little more closely."

"Understood, Chief."

"Thank you, Berger. If you've nothing else to do, you'd better get off."

"I'm starting the report, Chief. Tip will help me finish it after she's got that information for you."

"Fine."

Berger grinned. "After that, Chief, I could even go to Markies with her before going out for a bite and a drink."

"Some people have all the luck."

Berger glanced at him for a moment. "Hark who's talking, Chief. With a wife like Mrs Masters. . . ." The sergeant left without completing the sentence. He must have passed Tip in the corridor outside, for she entered immediately he had gone, almost breathless with excitement.

"Did you know, Chief?"

"That the cottage is in the name of Louis Packard, you mean?"

"Yes. How could you know?"

"I didn't know, Tip. I just thought it was a possibility. That's what I was thinking about when the DCI questioned me."

"He's owned it for more than two years, sir."

"Thank you. We'll talk it over tomorrow in the car on

97

the way to Ipswich. Please tell Berger I should like to leave here at nine."

"Right, Chief."

"Good night, Tip."

Wanda Masters had bathed and put her young son, Michael, to bed, and had then left the bedtime story telling to her husband while she busied herself with supper. The evening story was an on-going saga of a farm, worked and peopled by a large army of varied types, each one named, as were the animals. Woe betide Masters if he forgot a name. Michael never did. He was insistent that every one should come into the script every night. There were never any holidays for anybody on Strawberry Farm at any time of the year. Even Masters' inventive mind was sometimes so stretched to accommodate everybody easily, that he never dared introduce another character to help him out, otherwise the newcomer would become a permanent member of the cast, demanded inexorably by Michael.

Although he bemoaned the whips of his young taskmaster, Masters actually enjoyed the exercise. He was never quite sure whether it was the warm, baby-powder-perfumed company of his son or the exercise in fictional pelmanism that he found so much to his liking. But of one thing he was sure, and that was that if Michael really was absorbing all he was told—as he appeared to be— he would at least have a vast fund of general knowledge as a basis for later learning. And this pleased his father, not only because of the potential future benefits for Michael, but because it allowed him to introduce any and every subject. This day the farmer's wife, Mrs Strawberry, had installed a solarium in a spare bedroom because the summer had been so wet and cold she hadn't been able to get her usual suntan. Masters was able to use two or three minutes explaining what a solarium was and another two or three on the care that needed to be taken in handling the apparatus. Meanwhile, Fred the cowman and Ted the pigman were erecting a new fence with concrete posts and arris rails and Mr Strawberry was examining catalogues and Bobby Strawberry was mending the tractor and Freda, Fred's wife, was making jam. . . .

"I can hear you telling the story," said Wanda when Masters joined her after snuggling Michael down. "All except when I'm in the kitchen with the tap running."

"So you can take over when I'm away?"

She shook her head and stood on tiptoe to kiss his cheek. "No, darling. It's your story. . . ."

"And I'm stuck with it?"

"Not quite. Michael wouldn't like it nearly so much. My style wouldn't be the same. I listen to every word. This house is so small that any conversation can be heard if the doors are kept open and there's no tap running or TV playing. So I know all the characters and situations, and enjoy them. But Michael associates the people with you and I wouldn't like to break the relationship."

"So I hold the sole copyright?"

"I'm afraid so, darling. Do you think I could have a glass of sherry to take through to the kitchen with me? I've still got one or two things to do."

"Can I help? Lay the table perhaps?" he asked as he handed her the glass.

"That's all done. I did it very quietly while I was listening to the story."

Masters helped himself to gin and tonic and followed her through to the kitchen.

"George," she said, as she strained the cold water from a pan of potatoes preparatory to putting them into the water boiling on the stove. "You guessed that Packard owned Walesby Cottage. Why? I mean most people would simply assume he had a girlfriend there."

"Just so, darling. But I don't think I did guess, really."

"You mean you actually worked it out?"

"I like to think so."

"How?"

"The game of spot the difference that we decided to

play. The ordinary picture would have Packard going to Walesby Cottage, with a light o'love awaiting him. A temporary affair going on."

"Yes." She added salt to the boiling water.

"But I wondered if the picture I was comparing it with might not be different."

"No paramour basking in the nude on the solarium awaiting his pleasure?" She smiled at him. "You didn't bring out the fact for Michael that Mrs Strawberry, being a fat, jolly farmer's wife of middle years, might well have lapped over if she'd lain on the table."

He grinned back.

"Go on with the comparison," she urged, as she plopped the potatoes into the salted water.

"What if the difference was that there was no woman awaiting. What would be the purpose of Packard's visit?"

"To go to bed there alone instead of staying in an hotel?"

"Just so. Alone. Which meant that he either rented or owned the cottage for that purpose. Having got that idea, I went back to our hearsay evidence to see if I could support my idea. Mrs Packard was very certain her husband was not having an affair with another woman, nor that, like the sailor, he had a different woman in every port in East Anglia. I accepted that, simply because of the way she told it. She said she had to be prepared to be a wife in every sense of the word from Friday evening to Monday morning each week. It rang true. Besides, she is the type of woman who would be very bitter and vindictive if she thought her husband was being unfaithful, and she was neither."

Wanda said: "In that case I think you were right to believe her."

"Thank you for not saying the woman is always the last to know."

"Because I don't believe that is always true. But go on."

"So, point one. No woman at the cottage.

"Point two. Packard bought hotel bills, but never stayed in the hotels. So where did he stay? Answer, somewhere cheaper. What could be cheaper than one's own house?

"Point three. Rented or owned? Packard sounds to me to be the type who would want to buy his bricks and mortar, not pay to borrow them. So my vote is for ownership.

"Point four. How could he afford it? Answer, rake-off from fiddles over a few years would more than pay for it.

"Result? A good reason to suppose that Walesby Cottage was the property of L. Packard Esquire, man of means and nominally of Theydon Bois."

"Clever old thing, you. Open the plonk, darling. Bill and Doris will be here at any minute and the beef will be ready at any time."

"Beef?"

"Braising beef. Not a dirty great joint."

"I thought as much. Remarkable how eating standards are diminishing no matter how much one's salary goes up these days."

"Mother says she virtually lives on rabbits."

"All nicely caught and delivered free, no doubt."

"Why not. The local friendly poacher owes her a big debt and he's married to the woman who keeps house for her."

"In that case, why not pheasant?"

"That, too. In season. She's promised to bring us a brace sometime."

There was a ring at the front door.

"Talking of braces, that'll be a pair of Greens. I'll let them in."

"Don't tell me," said Green as he followed his wife into the tiny hall. "Berger rang me at home to say the girlie had discovered Packard owned Walesby Cottage but that you'd already sussed it out for yourself before she got the news."

"She confirmed what I thought, Bill."

"I wondered why you asked her to get the information.

101

I mean we could just have bowled along there tomorrow and knocked on the cottage door. But now. . . ." Green shrugged.

"We'll discuss it at table, Bill. Shall we join the girls and have a drink?"

The braised beef was very much to Green's liking. "Do you know, love," he said to Wanda, "this is first class. I've always preferred over-cooking to hob-cooking or grilling. What I mean is, these plates of meat . . ."

"Bill!" his wife expostulated.

"Now what have I said?"

"Plates of meat. When you say that you usually mean feet."

"Not this time, honeybun. I was referring to the shape of the pieces. They're not slices, exactly, they're like . . ."

"Tectonic plates," supplied Wanda, "though I suspect you mean lamina."

"If you say so, love. Anyhow, done like this in their own jizzer-rizzer, with all these little diced bits of peppers and carrots and whatnot, they're far better than lumps done under a gas flame or on charcoal."

"Thank you, William. I'm pleased you like the dish. George was a bit sniffy about it when he heard what I was preparing."

Green turned to Masters. "Grumbling, were you? At food like this?"

"Not quite, Bill. Wanda said we were having beef for supper, and I jumped to the conclusion she meant a roast of topside. She then told me she meant braising beef and I must admit I pouted a bit at the news. Not because I dislike braised beef. I like it very much. My moue of disgust was at the fact that, basically, Wanda and I cannot afford a good joint of roast beef these days. We could at one time, when my salary was a fraction of what it is today. And I'm not kidding. We really haven't had a joint of roast beef for over a year. Roast pork, roast lamb—lashings of it."

"We're the same," said Doris. "I just won't pay their prices."

"I'm pleased you weren't umpty about what your little missus has lobbed up," said Green, "because it's one of God's better inventions. I came to braised beef late in life, after I got married. We never had it when I was a lad. It was always roast or stews. Two sorts of stews, white or brown. Brown stew is now known as a casserole or by some fancy foreign name for a peasant food because they cut the meat in little thin strips instead of succulent chunks."

"White stew?" queried Wanda. "I don't know that."

"You wouldn't, love. If anybody attempts to make it these days they put a load of mutton chine-knuckles with all the meat taken off into a pot of boiling water and serve it up as lamb boulangere or some such. No, lass. White stew could have mutton in it—best end of neck or some such—but it also had bacon scraps. You know those packs you can buy of bits and pieces from the machine and the ends of joints? That goes in, too, with only white vegetables, like onions and celery. None of your gravy browning either. If you wanted it thickened, you did it with a bit of cornflour mixed with margarine and milk. My old mum used to slice her potatoes into scallops about a quarter of an inch thick and shove those in, too, towards the end of the cooking time. I'm telling you, love, it was just the job on a cold day."

"I'm sure it was. Pass your plate up, William. There's still some left."

"Ta."

"You've never told me about these white stews," accused Doris.

"I shouldn't have needed to, love. You should have guessed, like George did this afternoon." He thanked Wanda for his second helping and then turned to Masters. "Your cue, mate. Time for you to come in with all the revelations we're agog to hear. I shan't mind if you talk while I eat."

"You do say the most outrageous things, Bill."

"It's the fault of having been brought up on white stew, love. It has left me so pure, I'm naïve when it comes to manners." He waved his fork in the air. "Like pure, white snow, that knows no better than to look lovely and freeze your pipes at the same time."

Masters laughed. "I think we'd better carry on, Doris, otherwise we shall have more of this shining beacon in an evil world business to listen to."

"He's a silly ass," murmured Doris. "And a greedy one, too." She leaned across towards her husband. "And if you dare to ask me what a Greedy One Two is, I'll never bring you here again."

Fortunately, Green's mouth was too full to permit him to answer.

Masters explained again—for Green's benefit— how he had come to assume that Packard had bought Walesby Cottage. He finished by adding another factor in Green's report which had finally brought him to the belief that the rep had become the owner of the property.

"Packard was making some five or six thousand a year out of just two fiddles—the hotel bills and the petrol. There could well have been other bits of chicanery. Indeed, we know that he was defrauding Alpurplas to secure the price of free evening meals which, if you think about it, more than offset the money he was paying for buying hotel bills and the single gallons of petrol combined. So I estimate he was netting something like forty-three pounds per day, tax free, and that—counting only four hotel bills a week, but five fillings of petrol—would, by my reckoning, be one hundred and eighty pounds a week clear."

"Nearly ten thousand a year that we know of," said Green.

"Just so. But for how many years had this sort of thing been going on? Five or six years with Alpurplas and before then—but probably not in such a big way—for an even longer time with AVL. In other words, he has netted a considerable sum over and above his salary and bonuses, and yet, compared with such sums, he has comparatively small sums in his bank and building society accounts. So what did he do with the money? Nowhere are there any indications of his having lived it up."

"Answer," said Green, "bricks and mortar."

"Cash down," added Masters.

"Cash down?" asked Wanda.

"It had to be, darling, otherwise he would have left a trail we would have picked up by now. Just think. Had he taken out a mortgage on Walesby Cottage, he would have been receiving all manner of communications from the mortgagors. I know they would have sent them to the cottage, but if they hadn't had a reply or any repayments for six or seven months, they would have been asking questions."

"I see that, so how did he manage things so secretively?"

"Easy," said Green, pushing his empty plate away. "He opened up a building society account— with a different society from the one he used at home—and paid into it all his ill-gotten gains. He didn't give his home address in Theydon Bois, of course. He'd have the six monthly interest information sent to him care of his firm. Companies send their reps each week a large envelope full of all the literature they have to have. Letters addressed to him would reach him under that cover, so his wife would never suspect anything. He would open the envelope in private. After all, it was business literature and of no interest to his missus, so she wouldn't suspect anything. The only snag would be his income tax return, and that doesn't affect most people these days as the Inland Revenue only send them out to people they reckon have a second job or other sources of income.

"So, he piles up the loot until he has enough to buy the house he reckons he would like. And he buys it. Cash down. Now he has an address. Anything from his building society can be sent there with nobody being any the wiser."

"But what about other bills?" demanded Wanda. "Rates, water, phone, gas and so on?"

Green turned to Masters. "Your turn, chum. How are you going to get out of that one?"

"Fairly easily, I suspect. He probably has a bank account in the area with a few thousand in it. If he has signed bankers orders or whatever the new things are called . . . direct debits. . . ."

"That's it," said Green. "Estimated bills for electricity and whatnot because the meter readers couldn't catch him at home. You're right, George. No sweat. Until the bank account runs dry, of course."

"Which could be a long time. The phone bills, for instance will have no calls on them."

"But gas and electricity will be estimated, and estimates are always pretty high."

"Even so, I should think a thousand a year would cover things. The rates out there can't be very high."

"We're going to find mail a yard deep on that doormat when we go into the cottage tomorrow, George."

"I imagine so. I'm hoping it may yield us some information."

"How do you propose to get in?" asked Wanda.

"Back window," said Green laconically. "Berger is quite a dab hand at it." He turned to Masters. "And after Walesby Cottage, there's Kempe."

"True."

"Anything in mind concerning him?"

"Nothing. No, not true. There is something. Something we've heard during these last days, and for the life of me I can't recall what it was. It could be something quite trivial, but I have a nasty suspicion it could be important. I've tried to bring it to mind, but I can't. I have a feeling it was only a half-formed idea which I meant to return to and think out, but it has escaped me so far."

"You'll have to sleep on it, darling."

"It'll come," grunted Green. "They always do."

Wanda started to her feet with an exclamation. "Goodness, I've forgotten all about the pudding. Summer pudding actually. Can everybody eat that, made with raspberries and red currants?"

"Excellent," said Masters.

"Sounds lovely," said Doris.

"Couldn't be better," agreed Green. "Especially if there's a nice drop of cream to go with it."

5

"This will be a lot better when the M25 is finished," grumbled Berger, "then all we'd have to do is slip up the A10 and round till we hit the A12 at Brentwood. As it is. . . ." He applied the brake once more, and brought the Yard Rover to a halt behind the towering height of a juggernaut held up by roadworks in the Whitechapel Road.

"It'll be better once we get on Eastern Avenue," said Tip. "Going this way at least. Look at the mass going the other way."

Green, who had a pathological hatred of traffic, and who always sat in the nearside rear seat as being—to his way of thinking, at any rate—the safest in the car, was gripping the back of the seat in front of him so fiercely as to show up white and shiny the knuckles of his big hands. Masters, glancing at the set face of his colleague, showing fear being fought without the battle being decisively won, said quietly, "Take it easy, Berger, but make it as quickly as possible. And while we're stationary, take the opportunity to hand the DCI one of your cigarettes."

"No need for that, Chief," said Tip, half turning in her seat. "I brought some along." She opened the glove compartment and took out a new packet of Kensitas. "Just as a reserve," she added, stripping off the outer covering.

"But you don't smoke, Tip."

"Very rarely, Chief." She actually put the cigarette in her own mouth and lit it before handing it to Green, who managed to take one hand off the back of her seat to receive it. "But I've noticed that certain people who do smoke tend to run out at inconvenient moments. In conferences and . . . elsewhere."

"So you took it upon yourself to become a universal provider?"

"Not universal, Chief. I'd never presume to buy your tobacco." She glanced round at Green, concern on her face. "Just being a dutiful daughter to daddy."

The smile she gave him caused a response in Green. "You'll do, lass," he said gruffly. "And ta, muchly, for the fag."

By the time he had finished smoking it, the car was once more moving forward smoothly, with the traffic around them lessening as they passed the big buildings at the entrance to Eastern Avenue.

Green relaxed more and more as they sped towards Gallows Corner, and once the left turn up towards Chelmsford had been made he was, in Masters' estimation, fit to participate in the discussion he had promised Tip would take place in the car.

Berger and Tip listened as he gave a full and detailed report of the conference he and Green had held the previous evening.

"Any questions?" he asked when he had finished.

"Yes, Chief," said Tip. "Did you remember to bring a warrant for breaking into the cottage?"

"No need," said Green, more like his usual self. "We've found out that a missing man owns a house nobody else knew he had. We go there to pursue our inquiries and suspect from the look of the place that he's lying dead inside, somewhere. We don't have to have a warrant to go in and find him in those circumstances, do we? Act, and act quickly."

"Except that you know what we're going to do, and have known ever since last night. You've had plenty of time to get a warrant."

"True, petal, but warrants are there to protect people. That is, living people and their homes. We reckon Packard's dead. . . ."

"And do you really expect to find him dead in the house?"

"It's a distinct possibility."

Tip shivered slightly. "After six months he'll be . . ."

"Don't go on, love. I'm already feeling a bit below par. Before you've got very far with your imagined description of a six-month-old unburied corpse I'll have flung my pluck up, and that would make a nasty mess in the car for you to clean up, wouldn't it?"

Tip looked her reply, and if looks were words, what she had said to Green would have made a Glaswegian wino blush.

Masters intervened. "Although there is a chance we shall find Packard's body at his cottage, I feel there is an equal, or even bigger, chance that it won't be there. Dead bodies have a habit of proclaiming their presence, particularly if left above ground."

Berger groaned. "Not a garden search, Chief! Digging and probing and sifting."

"Not to worry, lad," said Green. "There's bags of water round there. Somebody could have dropped him in."

"Wait a minute," said Berger. "A couple of days ago when the Chief asked you about bodies in lakes and canals, you said. . . ."

"I know what I said, lad. But we were talking about what you might call inadvertent immersion. The same doesn't apply if somebody ties half a ton of pig-iron to your feet and drops you into a deep blob-hole."

Berger was about to expostulate when Green said, looking out the window, "I like this bit. A memorial avenue for the lads who died in the war. Good idea the Colchester people had, to dedicate a nice, straight, tree-lined avenue to those who didn't make it. Lovely trees. Almost meet overhead in places, even though it is a wide road."

"Not far to Ipswich now, Chief," said Berger quietly. "We'll be there by a quarter past eleven. Is this pub we're staying at in the centre of town?"

"No," said Tip. "I asked that. It's at the northern end

of Christchurch Park. We have to go on round the by-pass for about half a mile past the junction with the A1156 and then turn right."

"I think," said Masters, "that we shall be a little early to claim our rooms at The Blenheim, so we could go on to Debenham. When you get into the Ipswich area, please stop at any likely-looking pub or restaurant that advertises morning coffee."

After a cup of coffee in a pub bar, where Green had taxed his memory and their patience by trying to recall exactly what it was "his old mate Kipling" had written about avenues—presumably brought on by the Colchester memorial avenue which had affected him so much—in *The Glory of the Garden*, they took the B1077 north-wards and glided gently through the long village of Debenham.

"About a mile north, Emery said, didn't he?"

"Yes, Chief. But you know how deceptive distances can be at night. And don't go too much on it's being totally isolated. On a dark night a cottage twenty yards away can be invisible."

"I'll take this side," said Masters. "You take that side, Bill. There should be a name to help us if Emery saw one by night."

"There it is," cried Tip excitedly, pointing forward on the nearside. "Oh, what a sweet little place."

Masters peered forwards. The five-barred gate to the little drive was set back four or five feet behind the line of the hedge which curved in from both north and south to meet it. In both these quarter circles, so that they could be read, one from each direction, were the name boards. As Berger pulled up, Tip got out and opened the gate. As it swung back, the big car nosed in.

"Garage to the left," grunted Green as he descended. "What's the betting the car's in there?"

"I wouldn't bet against."

"With him in it?"

"Possibly."

111

"You mean you don't think he is."

"Shall we find out?"

Tip had been right when she had praised the look of the cottage, but wrong about the size. It was biggish, and not as old as the term country cottage so often implies.

"Edwardian," guessed Masters looking up at the windows. "I'd say at least four bedrooms and the paintwork is in pretty good nick."

"Padlock on the garage, Chief."

"Circle round and see if it has a window. We don't want to break in if there's no car there."

Berger and Tip disappeared through a wicket between garage and house. "Overgrown," grunted Green. "Nothing's been done to this garden this season."

Tip came running back. "It's there, Chief. Sergeant Berger says it's the Alpurplas car judging by the colour and make, but he couldn't see the front plate. But no body in it unless it's hidden in some way."

Berger joined them. "Shall I tackle the padlock, Chief?"

"If you can do it easily. If not, there's a chance there'll be a spare key inside the house."

"On a key ring on the body?"

"Not necessarily. We, for instance, keep spare keys in the little drawer of the telephone table."

Berger examined the heavy padlock. "It's a security job, Chief. Perhaps we'd better see if there's a spare indoors."

"Right. Try the front door. If that's locked, we'll go round the back. If we have to break in I would rather do it out of sight of passing motorists."

They decided to break a small window leading into a scullery to the right of the back door.

"I'll climb in," volunteered Tip. "I'm smaller than any of you. If you'll give me a leg up."

"Not in a skirt and nylons," said Masters firmly.

Tip looked abashed. "I'll wear corduroy slacks in future," she mumbled.

112

"I should, love. Not that any of us would object strongly to anything you've got to show, but His Nibs won't like signing expenses claims for 'tights, nylon, detective sergeants, female, for the use of.'"

After carefully removing the shards of glass, Berger was able to angle his body through the gap. A second or two later he was unbolting the back door. "It smells musty, Chief. But only from being shut up. There's no pong."

"Probably wouldn't be, even if the body's here," grunted Green. "Not after this long. But there'd be flies. Scads of 'em."

"I haven't seen or heard any."

They searched the house. It was easy enough to do. Only one bedroom was furnished, and the sitting room. The kitchen, apart from its appliances, had very few pots and pans. The refrigerator held a pack of bacon—still looking perfectly edible—half a dozen eggs in the door, a tub of margarine partly used and two separate litre cartons of orange juice. The bread bin had half a loaf of sliced bread covered in black mould, and on a working top was a selection of bottles and cans of drink, a bottle of powdered coffee and a tin of dried milk.

"As we suspected, he slept and had breakfast here, and that's about all."

"There's a lot of mail, Chief," said Tip.

"Right. Separate it into piles. Private mail, advertising shots, official stuff, if any, and then start reading it."

"Even the private letters, Chief?"

"Especially those. If there are any, that is. If Packard kept this place as much of a secret as we suspect, nobody would know the address to send him private letters, so don't feel so squeamish, young lady, and get going. I want to know if there's anything to interest us."

"Right, Chief."

Masters sought Green and Berger. "Found any spare keys?"

"Not yet," grunted Green. "I'm just going to look in the cupboard under the stairs."

"Chief, Chief?" Tip was on her knees among the mail just inside the front door.

"What is it?"

She held up a black key wallet. "This was underneath the heap of envelopes. Right on the door mat."

"Steady, steady," shouted Berger. "There could be prints on that leather."

"What? Oh, sorry. I'm afraid I've handled it."

"Do what you can with it, Berger," said Masters quietly, "and then see if the garage key is there."

"I've found a board in here," said Green, poking his face round the door of the cupboard under the stairs. "Half a dozen hooks with keys. Unnamed."

Berger was putting the key wallet in a plastic bag. "I don't think she'll have done any harm, Chief. I mean she won't have obliterated everything."

"Let's hope not."

Green had disappeared again. A faint glow from under the stairs suggested he was examining the keys by the light of a match.

"Anything that looks as though it would fit the garage, Bill?"

"I'm collecting them all. I'll bring them out into the light."

The key they wanted was there. The three men entered the garage.

"Unless he's in the boot, Chief, he's not here," said Berger.

Green was sniffing round the back of the car. "He's not here. No niffle. No flies."

"Still, we shall have to open up and have a look. I think we'll wait until this afternoon for that, because Berger will have to go over the wheel and things for prints."

"Somebody else brought it here, Chief?"

"Reckon so, lad," said Green. "Parked it here, locked up, and then shoved the keys through the front door letter box."

Masters nodded. "See if you can find something to block in the broken window, Berger." He turned to Green.

"See if you've got a spare front door key there, would you, Bill? If so, hang on to it. We'll go and come that way in future. I'll see how our young lady is doing."

Tip was on the sofa in the sitting room with several heaps on the floor at her feet.

"What have you found?"

"Nothing, Chief. It's just as you said. There's no personal mail at all. There are monthly bank statements and a new cheque book, but it doesn't look as though he had a Barclaycard with this account. At any rate there are no bills here. There are cards from the electricity and gas people to say they both called in January, April and June. There's a whole heap of free newspapers, and lots of things offering him double-glazing and central heating. And DIY catalogues. Scads of that sort of thing, but not a personal note from anybody."

"Right. Tidy up. It's time we were going back to Ipswich."

"Right, Chief."

Masters turned to the door.

"Chief?"

He waited. "Yes, Tip?"

"I'm sorry about the key wallet."

"Over enthusiasm, petal," said Green from the doorway. "You let it carry you away. You'll have to watch it."

Tip looked at Masters, who nodded to her as if to say he endorsed Green's stricture. "Come along," he said. "Get the car out on to the road while I see if Berger has finished making the place safe."

When the girl had gone through the now open front door Green said: "You were about to blast her, George."

"Not really."

"Oh yes you were. More than you would have done a male sergeant. Are you still sore at having to sign her on?"

Masters shook his head. "No. She's a bright girl. If I was about to tick her off as you seem to assume it was because she has so much potential that I want her to live up to it as soon as possible."

"For her own good, then?"

"I hope so."

"You know what it is, George. You have always felt you could rely completely on our two sergeants. With the little lady you're not sure. You're having to tell her, watch her, see how she goes about things. There's no need to, you know. She's a quick learner. You'll never have to tell her anything twice."

Masters grinned. "She has your vote, then?"

"A girl who makes sure I shan't run out of fags? I should just think she has. Which reminds me, I'll just go off and pay her for them."

A few minutes later they were travelling south towards Ipswich. After a little bit of guessing as to which was the correct turn to take off the ring road, Berger and Tip guided them to The Blenheim.

As soon as he entered it, Masters knew that The Blenheim was going to deserve the good report DCI Harold Knight had given it. Not too outstanding when looked at from outside, but immediately welcoming on entry. Compact. You could almost hear it saying that it had everything, and to hand. The reception clerk to the left of the door backed onto the front of the house, hidden from outside view by the depth of the porch. The foyer was a pleasant lounge with a fireplace full of flowers, coffee tables, easy chairs and settees. An open door to the right showed the bar to be a comfy place. The dining room, with a small table full of gorgeous cheeses outside it, was opposite the front door. The main staircase ran up, between the bar and the dining room, to a stained glass window. To the far left of the foyer an open way led to a conference room, the ground floor bedrooms, garden, car parks and second staircase for those more modern rooms which had been built on to the original house. For plainly that is what it had been. A big, family dwelling for wealthy people somewhere round the turn of the century when such places could be afforded and kept up.

And the staff. Young for the most part. Obviously carefully chosen not only for being personable but also for being pleasant and efficient with no hint of officiousness. The girl behind the desk had them sign in. The dark-suited manager, youngish, small and bespectacled was hovering there to help and to keep any eye on reception, bar and dining room. He it was who summoned help for carrying bags. It was the small, neat—and again, youngish—head waiter who appeared to ask if he should keep them a table for lunch.

And the rooms! When they assembled in the bar after having been shown their quarters, Tip came hurrying in, having changed out of a skirt into corduroy jeans, bubbling with excitement. "You should see my wallpaper. It's covered all over in Victorian Valentine cards. Really nice. All addressed to people with names like Miss Lucy Hopewell-Smith, and referred to as My Lady of Delight, whose features shine for ever bright, so fair in your admirer's sight. With ribbons and picture hats and flowers." She clasped her hands. "It's absolutely lovely."

Masters brought the drinks to the table in time to hear Green say, "They've given me bath essence, a shower cap and a housewife in a little basket. But the thing that really lights my candle is the fact that besides the spare shirt buttons, they've given me a needle threader. Now that, I think, is the height of sophistication. Never having seen one before, but having suffered with sucking the end of a bit of cotton to get it through the eye of a needle, I think I shall pinch it—accidentally on purpose, like."

Berger said: "They've put a bunch of sweet peas in my room."

"It's all very nice," said Masters, who didn't reveal the fact that he had been given the magnificent former master bedroom at the head of the stairs. He liked the furniture in there. Finely made mahogany pieces that would grace any home.

The manager appeared with an armful of menus. "You did say you would be having lunch, sir."

"We did," said Masters, "but only if we can have something very light. We've got work to do this afternoon, and I don't want us snoozing over the job."

"Anything you like, sir. The chef makes an excellent omelette. . . ."

With Tip driving, they dropped down into the centre of Ipswich, following a route cheerfully supplied to them by the receptionist, who warned them about one way routes and no-go areas for vehicles.

"Quite a bewildering town," said Masters. "They seem to have narrow streets and alleys, paper shops that look like Elizabethan houses, football grounds, docks, huge modern bridges and more churches per head of population than Tewkesbury has pubs."

"Wolsey," said Green laconically.

"Wot built 'Ampton Court?"

"The same. From what I can gather he was responsible for most of Ipswich."

"Not that tower block seemingly made of black glass, I take it?"

"The park area mostly," said Green, ignoring the interruption. "I read it in a brochure in The Blenheim. One of those they put in the big black folder on your bedroom table."

"Nothing like a bit of culture," grunted Berger.

"You could do worse than imbibe a bit, lad," grunted Green as Tip slowed down. "Ah, is this the local constabulary headquarters?"

"Probably built by Wolsey, too," murmured Berger as he left the car.

DCI Harold Knight was delighted to meet them. He was slightly flustered by Masters' presence at first, but once over the initial meeting he settled down and proved himself an efficient, co-operative colleague.

"No bother about Walesby Cottage," he said when he had heard about their visit there. "It's in our area, and though the man's disappearance has nothing to do with us on the face of it, officially I'm grateful to you for running to earth a stolen car."

"That's the ticket," said Green.

"However," continued Knight, "you did not unlock the

car or the boot. That will have to be done—for obvious reasons."

"Agreed."

"You say you have the key wallet with the car keys in it?"

"I have it, sir," said Berger. "I was going to dust it for dabs."

"You have only your travelling kit with you. If you let me have the wallet, I'll have it tested here and now on the premises. So if you would kindly get it from your car. . . ."

Berger looked at Masters, who nodded.

Knight, proving he was on top of his job, continued: "We'll lift some of Packard's dabs from the cottage for comparison and, I suspect, you would like me to get on to Colchester for the prints of this chap, Kempe, just to see if he has handled the wallet."

"I think that would be the right thing to do, but would you also ask your man to take Sergeant Tippen's prints, too."

"She's touched it?"

"Inadvertently. She was gathering up the mail from the doormat and the wallet was buried in the heap. Before she knew what it was. . . ."

Knight grinned. "She grabbed it and then realized she'd dropped a clanger." He winked at Tip. "Did the guv'nor bawl you out?"

"Not really," replied Tip. "He was icily nice about it."

"I can imagine. Off you go, then. Ask at the desk. They'll tell you and Sergeant Berger where to go to get the job done."

"Thank you, sir."

They waited until the door had closed behind Tip. "Icily nice, eh?" chuckled Knight.

"This is her first case with us," said Masters. "She joined us only three or four days ago, on promotion."

"Ah, I see. Well, I reckon she'll measure up in no time at all, sir."

"I'm sure you're right."

119

"Now, sir, about Packard. I take it you are convinced he's dead?"

"I should be very surprised if he weren't."

"So should I from what I've heard. But even after what you told me yesterday I had a general warning sent out—to uniform branch as well as CID—to keep their eyes and ears skinned for the car as well as the man. You never know, we just could get a hint of something. Now we've got the car."

"The man remains to be found."

"Or the remains of the man if he's been gone for six or seven months."

"Where's he likely to be, son?" asked Green.

Knight shrugged. "Underground? If so . . . well, we've got miles and miles of open space, wooded space, heathland and heaven knows what within our boundaries. It would be hopeless to initiate a search for him."

Masters took out his pipe. "I appreciate your point as stated. But did I detect a hint of reluctance to undertake a search? What I mean is, if you, quite properly, now wish to take over from us, you would feel obliged to . . ."

"Taking over from you is the last thing I want," said Knight. "Not that I want to duck any responsibility, even though the idea of a search for a buried body fills me with horror. No, Mr Masters. You are on the job. You've done all the preliminary work and it is emphatically your case. The fact that what you've learned so far has led you to our patch is no reason for us to take over from you. Why, in no time at all the leads may take you out of our area and into Orkney and Shetland for all we know. The cottage and the car are, however, firmly planted here in our bailiwick. So they are our responsibility, and so, with your agreement and co-operation, we will take that load off your shoulders."

"Just what I was hoping to hear. Would you like me to clear your suggestion with your Chief Constable?"

"Already done. I got in touch with my DCS this morning to let him know you'd been in touch and would probably come out here. He made no bones about it, sir."

"What did he say, son?" asked Green.

"'Harold, my boy, tell George Masters he can play in our garden as much as he likes. If he can handle a bit of serious trouble that would otherwise be down to us, why stop him? After all, he'll probably do it nearly as well as we would ourselves and I suspect Masters could do with the practice to keep him from going rusty.'"

Masters laughed.

"Honest?" asked Green.

"Slightly expurgated perhaps. For instance, the DCS also said that Mr Masters would as like as not bring with him an old colleague called Bill Green who had to be carefully watched if you didn't want all your fags to disappear smartish."

"Ah," sighed Green. "So my reputation runs ahead of me, too. But I tell you what, Harold, I could murder a cup of tea if there is such a thing in this wigwam."

They were half way through their cups of tea when Berger and Tip returned. Berger placed the key wallet on Knight's blotter. "No prints except those of Sergeant Tippen, sir. It had been wiped all over, even the keys, so you'll be able to take this for opening up the car without doing any damage."

"Thank you, Sergeant. There's some tea on the tray for you. I put the saucers on top of the cups to keep it warm, although in weather like this I don't think anything loses much heat."

A moment or two later Tip said to Masters: "The desk sergeant is getting us a town map, Chief."

"Good. It will save us asking The Blenheim receptionist the way every time we go out."

"How are you finding The Blenheim?"

"Not bad at all, Harold," said Green. "They've supplied me with a needle-threader and . . ."

Knight sat forward to interrupt. "Really? My missus has been trying to get hold of one of those for long enough. You don't think you could nick it for her, do you?"

"His is already earmarked," said Berger. "For his own

missus. You'd better have mine. But I'll not join the criminal classes. I'll offer to pay for it. It should cost all of 2p."

"I make them for Wanda," said Masters. "Out of fine fuse wire. I bought a pack of little lead seals and just put a loop through the holes before tightening up with a pair of pliers."

Green gazed at him hard. "You do what?"

"Make Wanda her needle-threaders."

"Good grief! And me wanting one for years."

They collected their map on the way out of the police station, and Tip again took the wheel. Ten minutes or so later they were at The Blenheim. Masters was last in the queue to collect his key. As she gave it to him, the receptionist said: "There is another guest, one who signed in this afternoon, who was asking where he could find you, sir. I merely said I thought you had gone into town. I hope that was all right."

"Perfectly all right. Who was this guest? Male or female?"

"It was the man who asked, sir. A Doctor Moller."

"Dr Harry Moller?"

"Yes, sir. As he was signing in he saw your names in the book and asked for you. He seemed very interested in your presence here."

Masters smiled. "Don't worry. He's not a policeman like us, but we have worked together several times. I shall be very pleased to see him."

"Oh, good, because we don't like . . . I mean, if you hadn't wanted to meet him. . . ."

Berger came up. "Excuse me, Chief, but I'm about to order a pot of decent tea. That we had down at the nick was half-cold and wishy-washy. Would you like some?"

"Yes, please. In about five minutes."

Berger turned to the receptionist. "Could we have tea for four down here in a few minutes, please? Nothing to eat."

"Right, sir. I'll have it brought out for you."

They used a long sofa table at the end of the foyer. Tip poured, and as she did so, she said to Green: "I've taken a leaf out of your book, Mr Green."

"There's nothing better you could do, petal. Which particular page have you pinched?"

"I've been studying the town plan we borrowed."

"Good. Not too much milk, sweetie. I like my tea brown, not white. That tea of Harold Knight's was good for neither him nor her nor anybody else as my old mum used to say."

"We're practically at the north end of the big park here, Chief."

"Christchurch?"

"Yes. There's a gate about a hundred yards away apparently, and the park runs right down into the middle of the town. It's huge. And down the west side—we're at the north-west corner—there's an arboretum. There are two lakes as well."

"Sounds as if it might be worth a visit," said Berger.

"The big house in the park was where Wolsey lived. It's a museum or something like that, now."

"There now," said Green. "History, culture, nature, all rolled into one. I'll take a gizz at this park after tea."

"We'll have an hour or so to spare before . . ."

Masters intervened. "I noticed you were careful to mention there were two lakes in the park. Got any ideas about them, Tip?"

"Not really, Chief. But they are there if you know what I mean. I expect they'll be terribly shallow and really quite small, but I thought you'd be interested to know of their presence."

"I am. They are almost certain to be as you've described them, but you were quite right to mention them. You should have done it a little more positively, though, not just hidden them in a list of horticultural attractions."

"Quite right," agreed Green. "Accentuate the positive, sugar. Any more tea in the urn? Squeeze the pot for me if you have to, love."

"Oh, by the way, everybody," said Masters, "Harry

Moller and his wife checked in here this afternoon."

"Did you know he was coming, Chief?" asked Berger.

"I had no idea. But he saw our names in the book and asked the receptionist whether we were in or out. I expect he just wanted to say hello."

"Who is Harry Moller?" asked Tip.

"Forensic scientist, petal," said Green. "Horseferry Road type. Sound sort of chap and clever as a wheel. He's worked directly with us a couple of times in the past."

"You say he's a government scientist?"

"That's right. Mid-thirties but quite senior. On the up and up. Doctor Moller."

Masters took out his pipe. "Is everybody coming to the park?"

All four of them went.

Tip led the way, accompanied by Berger. As she had told them, it was only a matter of a few yards to the junction where, in addition to the roads which joined at that point, there was a lane which could easily be overlooked by a motorist busy negotiating the turn. It was about twelve feet wide and metalled, with the high walls of properties on both sides and overhung by huge old trees.

"It's the back way in to these houses," said Green. "But there aren't any garage gates. Just wickets in the walls."

A couple of minutes brought them to the end of the walls, and at that point the park opened out before them. Straight on, the lane changed into a mere path, four or five feet wide, and ran through an iron gate into the arboretum which appeared to be a narrowish tract between the park proper and one of the roads leading from the Y junction. A board told them that the park gates were closed at sundown and opened at eight-thirty in the mornings except Sunday when the time was nine o'clock.

They turned left through a wider, open gate into the park. The first impression Masters had was how very well kept everything appeared to be. Acre upon acre of close-cut grass, rolling up quite sizeable hills and down into valleys through which, for the most part, led the paths. Clumps of trees stood up dark against the sheen of the grass, and close to the path which ran alongside the arboretum, beds full of vivid flowers.

"Floral route?" asked Masters.

Green grunted his agreement.

There was little conversation. As they went, the cultivated area opened out, and hidden among its byways and copses, they found little lawns, rockeries and more and more flower beds of every shape and size, with bench seats placed for those who wished to do so to sit and enjoy the view and the passers-by, of whom there seemed to be no shortage. Pensioners strolling, business men hurrying downhill after a day's work in their offices, their suits and briefcases striking an odd comparison with the brightly coloured clothes of young mothers with children and more mature women in flowered dresses and sun hats.

"This," said Green, "is right up my alley, George, but I'm very conscious of the fact that the general trend of these paths is downwards towards the town and we shall have to climb coming back."

Masters stopped. "Bill, why don't you sit on one of these benches in the shade? We'll pick you up on our way back."

Green's face brightened. "Now that's one of your better ideas, George. I'm not dressed for long walks in this weather and my shirt's sticking to my back."

"Over here," said Masters. He led the way across a lawn from the sunny side where they had been walking to a bench in the shade of the trees on the other side. "What about this, Bill?"

Green looked about him. "Couldn't be better. Just look at that, George." He pointed to a huge, towering tree that occupied a large part of the centre of the lawn they had just crossed. "You see that? They've had to prop its lower branches up on baulks of timber."

"It's a cedar of Lebanon, Bill. At the very least it is

hundreds of years old. And still in its prime."

"Not growing weak then?"

"I think not. It's just that those bottom branches are so very long and heavy that weight alone might break them off, particularly in rain or snow, because that foliage would catch and hold tons of the stuff. Another thing, I suspect, is that in a park like this they have to do it for safety. Those branches are absolutely horizontal and just at a height to appeal to lads for swinging on. The combined weights of two or three of them at a time could bring a nasty, probably fatal, crash. Let's face it, Bill. Those limbs alone are bigger than most trees."

Green sat down. "It's a sight for sore eyes," he said. "I could look at that all day." He glanced along the path. "Particularly if there's going to be a few bits of capurtle passing by every few minutes, like these two coming now."

Masters laughed. "You'll do, Bill. See you a bit later."

He hurried after Berger and Tip. For a moment or two he had been worried about Green. Never before had his older colleague hinted at fatigue. But the DCI's demeanour had reassured him. The heat of the afternoon sun, the unsuitable clothes he was wearing and the prospect of an uphill return the best part of a mile long would make any ageing man grasp at the offer of a seat as an alternative. Green was no fool. He'd foreseen what the discomfort was likely to be for him and so, before it was too late, he'd taken steps to avoid the toil and sweat.

Masters took left, jinking down small side paths, leaving a couple of bowling greens and several tennis courts on a small plateau on his right. Past a gardener's hut hidden by a grove of tallish bushes, a fenced-off nursery bed with last year's cuttings coming along nicely for next year, a small statue . . . as he went he marvelled at what could be hidden round corners. From the northern entrance none of these things had been visible, and yet one could have sworn the whole panorama was visible. At last he broke out into the open. The path he was following began to run down the valley, a re-entrant that carried just a purl of water that came up from the spring line and made no more of a stream bed than a brown furrow two inches deep and no wider than a gardener's spade. The water sped down, silvered by its ripples in the tiny confine. Ahead, Masters saw Berger and Tip. He quickened his long stride and saw them grow nearer by the second.

Berger looked over his shoulder and, on seeing Masters alone coming after them, stopped. Tip took a further step and then, aware that her companion was no longer with her, she too turned and stopped.

"Where's the DCI, Chief?" Masters noted there was a touch of anxiety in Berger's voice.

"Sitting down on a bench in the shade, admiring a magnificent cedar of Lebanon and such of the passing talent as takes his fancy."

"I can imagine," said Berger, now with a hint of relief. "We sometimes forget he's getting on a bit, Chief."

Masters felt unwilling to discuss the matter further and urged Tip, who was acting as guide, to lead on.

"The first lake is just ahead of us, Chief. The sun's wrong for seeing it properly, but I think this little stream feeds it."

Tip was right. For the last few yards, the stream was piped and ran under the grass to debouch into the lake. The configuration had made it impossible to recognize as a lake against the bright glare of the sun. The water was hidden from their viewpoint by an island, separated round its northern, eastern and western flanks by a narrow channel scarcely four feet wide, its surface well below the banks. The rise of the island, densely wooded not only with trees but also with bushes and other undergrowth had given a foreshortened view. They saw the lake open out on the far side of the island as the path brought them close and led to a wider concourse on its southern side.

"Plenty of ducks," said Berger, as a small convoy sailed

towards them in the hope of being fed. "Just look at the sheen on those blue and green feathers near their heads."

"Any idea what they are?" asked Tip.

"Several sorts," replied Berger. "And I don't know any of them."

Masters from a couple of yards ahead said: "There's a board here with all the different makes on."

"Illustrations as well," exclaimed Tip. "Oh, how lovely. Don't they look beautiful." She half leant over the guard rails surrounding the pond the better to examine the board which was planted a yard or so inside them. "Black-headed gull, Moorhen—they're the little ones— Mallard, Mandarin duck—I can't see one of those—red-crested Pochard—he's pretty—and Tufted duck—they'll be the ones with that little quiff on top."

The men joined in her enthusiastic identification of the birds and watched as they went up the tiny boards placed at intervals to allow them easily to leave the water and climb on to the island. "Look at them," said Tip, "just sitting there."

"They seem to have their own little areas there," said Berger. "Just the bare patches near the water. They don't seem to penetrate the undergrowth at all."

"What I've noticed," said Masters, "is that what I've always known as duck-boards are nothing like those little ramps. Those boards are solid, with little struts across . . . look at that one waddling up. If there'd been gaps he'd never have made it."

"He is a bit of a barrel, isn't he, Chief? I expect they're all grossly overfed. Look, over there, there's a child feeding a group of them on currant buns."

They crossed this broader bit of road to look over the opposite rail where the overflow from the pond came underground into a little splash basin.

"That's not the second of the ponds, is it?" asked Berger.

Tip consulted the map she was carrying in her shoulder bag. "No. It's over there, somewhere, a bit nearer the house."

"I can see it," said Masters. "This way."

It was not far. This time the lake was circular and somewhat ornamental, without the overgrown island, but with a bank area designated for the ducks within the fence.

"Same species," said Berger, reading the board.

"Time we were getting back," said Masters. "But if we get the chance I'd like to see more around here. There's still a lot left between here and the town."

"There's the arboretum, too, Chief, and a dirty great statue in the middle of about three acres of lawn."

Masters agreed and they turned to retrace their steps. When they reached Green, Tip sat down beside him and said: "When we come again, I'll take the car round by road and park it at the main gates at the bottom. Then you can walk all the way downhill and have a lift home. You'll love seeing it all. It's very pretty."

"Thanks, lass, and what will you do?"

"Just walk back to meet you, of course."

Green looked up as two girls in very abbreviated, washed-out and cut-off jeans, walked past, their long, suntanned legs as perfect as one could wish to see. "You know, love, I'm not at all sure I'd not be better just sitting here. The scenery's beautiful."

"Oh, men!" groaned Tip, standing up.

"What about us, petal?"

"You're all the same."

"Be honest, love, you wouldn't like it if we didn't fully appreciate a bit of natty underpinning when we saw it, would you?"

Tip refrained from answering. Masters said, "Come on, Bill. If we want a drink before dinner. . . ."

"Say no more," said Green, getting to his feet. "Lead on, you young 'uns."

Masters had just got out of his bath when there was a

knock at his bedroom door. Clad only in a bath sheet round his middle he opened it. A young waiter stood there with a tray on which were several schooners of sherry.

"Compliments of the management, sir. Would you care for a sherry? Medium only, I'm afraid."

"Please don't apologize for only having one sort," said Masters, taking a glass. "Do you do this for all your guests?"

"All of them, sir, on the first night of their stay with us. It is the manager's way of welcoming people."

"What could be better than that."

Masters drank his sherry as he dressed in a very thin, light grey suit. Wanda had insisted that he should provide himself with one or two of them when she guessed, somehow, much earlier in the year, that the summer would be long and hot. He had never discovered how his wife knew in advance that there would be a need for tropical suits that summer but he blessed her for her foresight and prescience.

"Not bad," said Green as Masters joined the others in the bar. "A buckshee glass of sherry and now these." He held up two or three little savouries which he held in one hand. "The lass from the kitchen brought a trayful round a few minutes ago, offering them. I took two or three."

"So I see." Masters looked round him. "This is rather nice. Not crowded and everybody seated on bar stools or at round tables. Very civilized."

"She knows to bring you a drink when you got here," said Green. "It's that sort of place. You can lay things on. Ah! Here it comes. Gin and tonic with ice and a slice. All right?"

"Perfect," said Masters, accepting the drink. "I wonder if Harry Moller's coming in for dinner."

"No, you don't," said Green. "Except for a chat. There's nothing here for you and him to go into a huddle about. He's on holiday with his missus, and she won't want forensic discourses even if you two do."

"I promise to be good," said Masters.

"No brainstorming tonight, Chief?" asked Berger.

"I think not. We'll go off after breakfast to see Kempe." He turned to Tip. "Have you found his place on the street plan?"

"I've marked both streets, Chief. Home and restaurant."

"Thank you. We'll try the restaurant first. If they serve breakfasts they'll be at work before we are."

"By the way, George," asked Green, "have you remembered whatever it was you thought you ought to but couldn't?"

"Say that all again," said Berger. "Slowly, so that we can understand."

"Somewhere along the line, lad, His Nibs thought he got a hint of something, but he was otherwise engaged at the time, so he did not mentally pin it down. Now it has escaped and he can't recall it."

"He will," said Berger confidently.

"He's got a memory like an elephant, you mean?"

"Have another drink before you allow yourself to answer that, Sergeant. What's it to be?"

It was while Masters was at the bar that Harry and Mrs Moller entered. Moller was a spare figure of a man, quite tall, with good shoulders. The skin of his face and hands was naturally brown, as if permanently suntanned, while his dark, wavy hair was now beginning to show flecks of grey. He was, in all, a handsome man, but without arrogance. His wife, whom Masters had never met before, was somewhat older than Tip, more squarely built than her husband, with a jolly, rather than pretty face. When she shook hands, her grip was firm and her smile charming, being carried in the eyes as well as on the lips.

After introducing her to Masters, Moller took his wife across to meet the other three at the table. "Pleased to meet you, Celia," said Green. "Does he treat you well, or does he put everything you say and do under that microscope of his?"

"Just the opposite. He can never see or find anything at home. I call him Sam, sometimes, because his vision's limited."

"I know," said Green. "He can't see through a flight of stairs and a deal door. All husbands are like that. Just keep him away from George Masters and you'll enjoy your holiday."

"I'm sure we shall. We've been here several times during the hotel's summer cheap period. It's a lovely base and a good centre for getting about. I'll make sure I get Harry well away every day."

"Shame," said Moller.

Masters came up with the drinks. "Harry," he said, "I'm pleased you've come, because . . ."

"There you are," said Green, "What did I tell you?"

"I was only going to say that the sight of him had recalled something I was trying to remember."

"OK," said Green. "Tell us."

"No shop," said Masters. "You've been saying so, haven't you?"

Green was about to reply, but at that moment the manager arrived with the menus.

6

"What are you going to say to those two?" asked Green as Tip drove them towards the Kempes' restaurant.

Masters grimaced. "There's not much I can ask, except to get them to talk about Packard."

"They'll love that, being under the impression he sent Alan Kempe down for three years, after having killed a girl in his name."

"I know bringing it up again won't make them very happy, but we've got to do it."

"We?"

"You and I. I think four of us would be a bit of a crowd if the Kempes are busy."

"Fair enough." He leaned forward in his seat. "What's happening now?"

"I shall have to park here," said Tip. "We can't get the car near the restaurant. It's not far. Just up the lane, across the road, down the lane opposite, and . . ."

"You be careful, or you won't get any pudding for dinner," replied Green.

"What a pity! And they have such a nice trolley at The Blenheim. But there, you should know. What was it you said to that young waiter last night? 'I can't make up my mind, son, so give me a cocktail of two or three profiteroles, a wedge of gateaux and likewise with the apricot flan'? And you had it topped off with cream."

"Well," said Green. "That half duckling I had wasn't very big, nor was the seafood omelette for starters."

"I know. After he'd had the omelette, Dr Moller cancelled his pheasant. He was already full."

133

"He ate too many of those savouries in the bar before we dined."

Tip pulled the parking brake on. "Anybody got any change for the pay and display?"

They found The Capercaillie Restaurant without any trouble.

"Nice looking place," said Green. "Pretty upstage, like Harold Knight said."

Masters led the way in. The dining room was on two levels, the upper half, with a bar, just two steps up from the lower half. Long steps, running the length of the room, covered in the same turkey carpet as the floors. These were the colours picked up in the draperies and chair covers. The tables had white starched cloths, cut glass vases of sweet peas and cutlery that gave the impression it was made of silver. A girl in a beautifully ironed cotton frock and nice sandals came towards them.

"Breakfast, sir?" she asked Masters.

"No, thank you. I would like to see Mr Kempe if he's here."

"Mr Kempe isn't here, sir. He's gone off to supervise a marquee being put up for a golden wedding party tomorrow."

"Mrs Kempe?"

"She's in the office. I'll ask her if she can see you."

"Impress upon her, please, that she must see me. I'm a policeman."

"And a very senior one," added Green.

"Right, sir. Would you come this way, please?"

The office lay between the restaurant and the kitchen. It had been built to occupy half the width of the gap, but situated in the middle, so that those entering the kitchen went down the left side, while those coming out used the other. The room was of polished mahogany for the bottom four feet of its walls. Thereafter it was of glass except for the last foot or so up to the ceiling. Masters found himself thinking that if Annabel Kempe had caused this to be built to her own design, she must be a shrewd woman. Anybody sitting in that office could see exactly what went on in the kitchen, what came out of it, and what went on in the restaurant.

"Two policemen to see you, Mrs Kempe."

Masters would have liked to see the effect of this announcement on Mrs Kempe, but her face was hidden by the body of the girl.

"*Two* policemen, Debbie? Did they say what they wanted?"

"Only that they are very senior policemen and insist on seeing you. They asked for Mr Kempe first."

"I see. Show them in, Debbie, please."

"My name is Masters, Mrs Kempe. I am a Detective Chief Superintendent from Scotland Yard, and this is Detective Chief Inspector Green." Masters produced his identity card and held it well forwards towards her, ostensibly so that she would be able to read it, but really so that he could get a close look at her eyes to see if they showed any reaction at the sudden appearance of two senior detectives.

"What can I do for you?" She remained in her seat and spoke quietly.

"Invite us to sit down, first off, love," said Green. "We must look untidy standing up."

Green's remark was not far from the truth. There was little room to spare for two large men in the spare space of the office.

"Help yourself."

Masters thought that Mrs Kempe was not readily going to afford them much help. Perhaps her previous experience of policemen had left a bitter impression. Perhaps there were other reasons.

"We came primarily to see Mr Kempe."

"Why bother with me, then?" She was sure of herself, this one. Dressed in a navy linen dress with heavy white saddle stitching and the hint of a nonchalantly-tied white bow at the neck, she was well turned-out, and she knew it. Her hair was dark and heavy, cut across the brow in a square fringe and then page-boyed into the sides and back. Very businesslike. And her face, by no means that of a beauty, had a look of competence about it. The sort of face, Masters guessed, that would not smile easily—one for which a conscious effort would have to be made to register amusement or tenderness or any of the happier emotions.

"We thought perhaps you might be able to give us some of the information we would like."

She waited for him to continue. Self-assured.

He led straight in. "Some years ago your husband was convicted of the manslaughter of a young girl."

"Wrongly convicted is the correct answer to that if it was meant as a question."

A strong reply, but nevertheless one hand had stayed on to the desk to finger a pencil, before she continued: "Are you here to tell me that you have at last realized the police made a mistake?"

"For you, or your husband, to tell us why you believe the police made a mistake."

She glanced at him shrewdly before saying: "The evidence was planted on him—I believe that is the term you use when such things are fixed by a third party."

"What third party?"

She didn't answer.

"You have no idea as to whom the third party could have been?"

"No."

"I see."

"Oh, come on, love," intervened Green. "As we understand it, your husband's car was discovered with a buckled wing and other damage. The paint from his car matched the flinders found on the girl's body. He had driven alone along that road at the time the girl was killed. How could all or any of that evidence be fixed?"

"I have my husband's word for it that when he garaged his car at home his car was undamaged."

"And you believe him?"

"Most certainly."

Masters came in again. "You believe that somebody

136

removed a sound offside wing from your husband's car and replaced it with a damaged one?"

"I do."

"A tricky operation to carry out, stealthily, at night, with the electrics and other connections to be made good."

"Nevertheless that is what happened."

"And you expected the police—in the face of such evidence—to take your word, and that of your husband, that he had not been involved?"

"Yes."

"Did you tell the police at the time that the wing had been changed?"

"No."

"Why not?"

"Because it didn't occur to us. We thought the car had been taken out in our absence. My husband had not locked the garage and we, with two guests, went out to dinner in their car. My car was in for maintenance. We were away for the best part of four hours. We assumed that during that time the car had been stolen, involved in an accident and then returned."

"But that would have meant the timings were wrong. That the girl had been killed far later than she actually was."

Annabel Kempe shrugged. "I knew the police had made a mistake in suspecting my husband. Why shouldn't they have made a mistake over the times?"

"Hardly likely, was it, love?" asked Green. "Not with medical evidence as to the time of death. . . ."

"Notably inexact," retorted Mrs Kempe.

"But when she was found, and the ambulance went for her . . . those times weren't even down to the police. They were exact enough."

"In our state of mind at the time we were slightly less rational that that."

"So you are saying," said Masters, "that the police timings were not wrong?"

"I am, now."

"How soon did you come to that conclusion and change your opinion of what happened?"

"Days. Weeks, perhaps."

"But in time to give the revised story to your husband's solicitor and barrister before his trial?"

"Yes."

"What was their reaction?"

"They built the defence round it."

"And failed. Why?"

"What do you mean, 'why'?"

"Did they not ask for a forensic and mechanical examination of your husband's car by experts of their own choosing? People who could tell that the nuts had been loosened and then done up again, that the mastic was new?"

"By the time we got round to that there was no hope of such an examination. The police had removed the wing and shattered lights. Those were the only parts they kept as material evidence. The car belonged to our employers and they had asked for it back to renew the necessary parts so that it could go back into service. Of course the bolts looked as if they'd been recently removed because they had, by the police."

"And the mastic remained supple?"

"It was a fairly new car."

"Quite. Had you any idea of who might have exchanged the wings?"

There was a momentary pause.

"No."

"A pity. Had you had a name to give the police they would have looked into it, you know."

"We had no name to give them. How could we have had?"

"Quite easily, I'd have said."

"How were we to know who could have stolen the car?"

"But you suggested a short time ago that the car had not been stolen. Merely that its wing had been changed for another."

"Very well. How were we to know who might have changed the wings?"

"Is it a question of *might* have changed? Isn't it, rather, who *could* have changed them?"

She put her hands, palm down, on the desk in front of her, in a gesture of controlled anger. "Look, I don't know where this conversation is getting us. What happened, happened. It is all water under the bridge. All I want to do is forget it."

"Do you?" asked Masters. "You don't want the record set straight?"

"What good would that do? My husband was convicted of a crime he didn't commit and sent to prison for it. It blasted our lives. He lost his job, and when he came out he couldn't get another. Ex-prisoners do experience that difficulty, you know. So we set up here with what capital we could scrape together. He and I have worked hard, both in an effort to forget the past and to make a success of this business. We've managed both, thank God."

Masters nodded. "It looks to be a thriving place, and if it's of any interest to you, I have heard good reports of it."

"Thank you." It was a bitter reply.

"It wasn't the worst way in which to be forced to change your lives, love."

She laughed mirthlessly. "I suppose you expect me to accept that it's an ill wind etcetera?"

"Something of the sort," agreed Green.

She leant forward, hands still on the desk, her eyes angry and her cheeks flushed. "Let me tell you something, Mister Green. When I got married it was because I loved a man and wanted not only him, but his children, too. When my husband was convicted, I was pregnant with what was to be our first child. When he was sent to jail, I had an abortion. Why? Because there is no life in this society of ours for a child whose father is an ex-convict. And don't try to deny it and say we *are* fairer than that. We're not. How fair is a society that convicts an innocent man and imprisons him for years?"

"You didn't help it to be more fair," said Masters quietly.

139

"And what do you mean by that?"

"Your husband worked for AVL, and so did you. There were scores of you—reps—all with exactly similar cars from the same fleet. The same age, because they were all changed together every two years. Furthermore, on the day that girl was killed by a hit-and-run driver in a car of the same make and colour as those you AVL reps drove, a great many from the AVL fleet all left Harwich at almost the same time; that is, not long before the girl was killed and only a few miles from where those cars started their various journeys."

"What about it?"

"Surely it must have occurred to you that the car which killed the girl probably came from among those AVL cars."

"I don't see why it should have done. Red Cortinas are not the rarest cars on the road."

Masters ignored the reply. "And if it was an AVL car which killed the girl, then it was presumably an AVL driver. If not your husband, which of them could it have been?"

"How would I know?"

"Perhaps you could have worked it out by a process of elimination."

"Meaning what, exactly?"

"As I understand it, most of the cars carried three or four people. A nasty business like killing a girl on the road would be very difficult to keep quiet if there were a number of witnesses, wouldn't it?"

"Maybe."

"Let me assure you, from experience, that a secret shared is not a secret halved, but a secret broadcast."

"Go on."

"Some of the cars—not many perhaps—carried one person only. The driver. Your husband was a case in point, I believe. Wouldn't you suppose that a single person was most likely to be the guilty one?"

"You tell me."

"I think it is likely to have been the answer you were

so desperately seeking at the time. A lone driver with a known ability to repair cars with the skill of a professional mechanic. Did such a solution never occur to you?"

"No."

"Think, please. Was there a person who would have fitted that description and whom you could have mentioned to your husband's defence lawyer if not to the police?"

She leant back and smiled, artificially sweet. "We never considered such a person, Mr Masters, even if one existed unknown to us. You see, we thought the changing of a wing from car to car, undoing two and bolting two up again together with other adjustments would take at least two, three, or even four men. In fact, when we thought things over we discounted any of our colleagues who had travelled alone. If there were any, that is. I wouldn't know if there were, because we never asked."

"I see. So there is no name you can suggest to us of who might have been guilty of—as you yourself put it— fixing the evidence against your husband?"

"I can think of no one."

Masters rose. "In that case, we won't waste any more of your time, Mrs Kempe."

"Please don't go without telling me why you came."

"We just happened to be passing," said Green.

"That," said Mrs Kempe, "is about what I would expect of a policeman. They either tell you nothing or they tell lies. You'll be able to find your own way out, won't you? I can watch you go out of the door from here."

"Have you two been anywhere near that restaurant?" demanded Masters when they met Berger and Tip almost as soon as they were outside.

"Not really, Chief. Sorry, but I thought you would rather we kept in the background."

"Quite right. Now Tip, you know where the Kempes live?"

"Yes, sir."

"Take Mr Green there as quickly as possible." He turned to Green. "Keep observation there, Bill. I'd like to know if she calls her husband to meet her there. Don't do anything. And keep out of sight."

Green stared at him. "Something on your mind, George?"

"No matter how hard I pushed her to do so, she steadfastly refused to mention Packard's name."

Green nodded. "I think I know what you think that implies. See you at lunchtime. Come on, lass, we've got to jazz the cans."

When they were gone, Masters said to Berger. "I shall wait here, just round the corner of this alley, so that I can keep an eye on the front door of the restaurant. I want you to work your way round to see if there is a back entrance. Fairly quickly. Keep an eye open. I want to know if a woman in a navy blue dress with white stitching on it, and a white tie sort of thing at the neck, comes out and goes off. She's got dark hair. Rejoin me in an hour from now if nothing has happened by then."

Masters lit his pipe soon after Berger had left him. He felt far from pleased at having to keep observation, a chore which even the most junior policeman found irksome. But to counterbalance his dislike of the job, he felt quite happy about the outcome of the interview with Mrs Kempe. As he had remarked to Green, Annabel Kempe had been at pains not to mention Packard's name. Had stressed, in fact, that they had never been aware that he had left Harwich alone in his car on the day of the hit-and-run. This must be nonsense. The sales director of AVL knew and, according to him, so did all Kempe's colleagues in the field force of those days. And all the reps knew that Packard was a highly skilled car mechanic. The idea that Packard—with a reputation as hard as granite—was implicated must have occurred to Alan and Annabel Kempe, even if it had not been mentioned to them by other reps. So why steer clear of a name surrounding which there was so much suspicion? Masters read it as meaning that the name Packard was looming too large in Annabel Kempe's mind at the moment to permit her to mention him. Some inner sense was telling her to steer clear of the name in the vain hope that the police would not connect her with it if they didn't hear it from her lips.

Or so Masters thought, as he drew on the pipe of War-lock Flake that was burning so evenly on this pleasant summer morning. And if what he thought was right, it meant that Annabel Kempe—if not her husband, as well—knew something about Packard: had seen him in the not too-distant past, and was aware that whatever knowledge they had of him was not for police consumption. And that meant what? Criminal connotations? Had they been so desperate after Kempe's release from jail and his failure to get a job that they had somehow come into contact with Packard and asked him for backing? The backing of dishonest money? The supply of stocks that had fallen off the back of lorries at dirt-cheap prices? Bogus luncheon bills for some of his sales schemes? Anything that put them in his debt and which they suspected of being outside the law? Criminal activity which could send down Kempe, already a convicted man, for a good long stretch? A stretch he would not find congenial and would do his best to avoid? A feeling which his wife shared: a feeling which drove her studiously to avoid mentioning Packard's name to the police lest news of the connection should leak out? If so, what were their thoughts about Packard not having been about this last six months or so?

This was as far as he had got when he saw Berger coming towards him at a fast walk.

"She took a taxi, Chief. Thank heaven she did. She obviously had to wait a few minutes for it to arrive, otherwise I'd have missed her. Or if she'd taken the little van which was round the back. Nicely painted little job with just The Capercaillie and no names painted on it. Not as big as a baker's van. One of those little snub-nosed Honda jobs. Handy for taking trays of cakes and with sliding doors at the sides as well as at the back."

"She was in a hurry?"

"I think she was, Chief. She skipped out as soon as the cab arrived and ducked in smartish. I've got the name of the taxi firm and its number if we want it later."

"Excellent. In that case we're no longer wanted here. Apart from this restaurant, have you seen one where we could get a cup of coffee?"

"There's a cake shop, Chief. . . ."

"What could be better? Which way?"

After they left the cake shop, Masters seemed to want to wander round the centre of Ipswich. He stopped to look in shops and to stare at buildings until finally he said: "Nearly twelve o'clock. If we can find the south end of the park, we can walk up through it to The Blenheim."

"No sweat, Chief. I've got a second town map in my pocket." Berger took it out and opened it. After looking about him for a moment or two, he put his finger on a spot. "We're about here. If we make our way up to the local bus station just here, and then turn right for a few yards. . . ."

"Got it," said Masters. "Not very far at all. Young Tip was right when she said that dropping down through the park would be almost as quick as driving into town."

Berger said: "It's very compact, actually, Chief. The town, I mean. I know the railway station and the football ground and so on are out on the fringes, but the town centre itself is very concentrated. Really, if you lived here long enough to find your way about, you'd find everything within spitting distance. Baths, hospital, scads of churches, all kinds of shops . . ."

"And the park entrance," suggested Masters. "Here we are. Big gates this time. Much more impressive." He stopped and looked about him before moving a few steps to his left. "Ah, yes. I've got it. The arboretum entrance is just up this side road a few yards." He returned to the main entrance and surveyed the house, standing back behind a huge lawn. "Wolsey's pad, as the DCI would put it. Very nice. Refreshment van handy for people coming in. And a row of benches flanking the drive."

"Well patronized, too," said Berger. "It looks as though most of the pensioners in Ipswich come here to sit in the sun and gossip."

As they walked up the tarmac drive between the row of seats and the trees opposite, Masters said: "I'm intrigued by this park."

"You reckon it's pretty good, Chief?"

"I do. I'd say it would be a distinct asset to any town. It's beautifully kept without being stuffy or formal. As you can see, the old can sit and snooze, others of us can stroll amid the pleasantest of surroundings, and the young can play on nice short grass. There are some youths over there chasing about, but the place is so vast you can't even hear them, and they are disturbing nobody."

Berger dropped back behind Masters to allow free passage to two young mothers pushing their prams abreast and occupying most of the roadway. Masters halted to allow the sergeant to rejoin him.

"There's the smaller of the two lakes, just ahead, beyond the museum. Where we were yesterday."

"Watch out for the van, Chief."

"Yes, thank you. I've noticed one or two vehicles running about. Gardener's lorries and the like."

"There's a row of cars parked near the house," said Berger, "and I don't know whether you saw them, Chief, but there are a number of . . . well, I suppose they're gardener's houses . . . dotted about, and they've got cars and garages."

"Houses?" asked Masters.

"Yes, Chief. Hidden away, almost. There's one at the main gate, of course, but I think I've seen at least two, round behind copses."

"So some of the staff live on the job, do they?"

"Looks like it, Chief. In fact, they'd have to, wouldn't they? Somebody's got to be here to lock the gates last thing at night and unlock them again in the morning."

Masters said nothing for a minute or so as they rounded the first lake and headed across to the larger one. "How many gates are there, Sergeant?"

Berger thought for a moment. "At least five that I know of at the moment, Chief. We've used two to the park itself, and seen two to the arboretum. I noticed a fifth yesterday, which opens on to the road near the big school they've got here. Just an ordinary wooden little gate. I seem to remember it was fairly newish. But they're all on the western side of the park. Whether there are any others on the eastern side or not, I don't know. But if it's important . . ."

"Not really. Does the map show the gates?"

"Hang on a moment, and I'll have a look."

Berger knelt to open the map on the grass.

"No gates shown, as such, Chief. But the paths in the park are dotted in, and where they reach the boundary in the places we know of, there are gates. So I expect there's an entrance on the north-east side where two paths converge." He got to his feet and folded the map.

"Thank you," said Masters, absentmindedly.

They began the gentle climb through the main, vast area of the park. Here they were in the open with the great downland hill on their right. People reclined on its grassy slopes, others walked the little brown tracks that wound upwards to the summit. Lots of people and yet lots of room. This was what Masters liked about it. Lots of space and yet no solitude. His eyes kept wandering to his left: to the copses, with their lawns, flower beds, paths, tennis courts, sheds and statuary, all hidden from their present route. And Berger had said there were houses in there. The map had even shown one path crossing underneath another via a short tunnel: a feature nobody could expect and which would have to be sought for by anybody wanting to see it. And all so many years old. Basically this was Wolsey's garden, changed in detail over the years, perhaps, but, he guessed, still in a form that would have been recognizable to the Cardinal: the trees, some of which would have been old in the first half of the sixteenth century, still standing in this latter half of the twentieth to provide this haven of peace and pleasure for young and old.

"All right, Chief?" asked Berger.

"Perfectly, thank you."

"You were looking a bit . . . well, I suppose you'd call it pensive."

"And what would you call it?"

"I don't know. Not day-dreaming, exactly, but certainly whatever it was had taken you a long way away. You weren't with us, as the DCI might say."

"Wrong, Sergeant. I was very much right here."

"In that case, Chief, the thoughts you were busy with were not very funny ones. You looked a bit frowny to me. I wondered if the hill and the heat were getting a bit too much for you."

Masters laughed out loud. "For me? This? I don't think I even realized we were climbing."

The path they were following turned left and a minute or two later they were walking the side of the pleasance where Green had rested the previous afternoon. From there it was only a few minutes' walk to the gate they had first used.

"They fence off that top bit for exercising dogs," said Berger. "Nice idea that. A good space for them to run, with no risk of fouling the rest."

"Bad luck on the householders whose gardens back on to it if the dogs start barking."

"No, Chief. I shouldn't think the dogs give them any trouble at all."

"I suppose not." They left the park and walked up the little alley towards The Blenheim. Berger was wondering about Masters. For the last half hour or so he had been totally unlike his usual self. And that remark about the siting of the dog-exercising enclave being bad luck on householders had been just so much rubbish. But Masters didn't talk rubbish or make irrelevant remarks, not the sort that he would immediately acknowledge as erroneous with a simple, "No I suppose not" as he had done just now. Berger decided to consult Green about it. The DCI usually knew what bees were buzzing around Masters' bonnet.

"The car's parked in front of the hotel, Chief."

"So it is. Would it be too much to hope that they've lined up a drink for us?"

Green and Tip were, unexpectedly, sitting in the foyer, reading newspapers.

"What's all this, then?" demanded Berger. "Sitting out here when the door of the open bar is not six feet away! What I've lived to see!"

Green looked at him over the top of a tabloid. "You've got to remember, Sergeant, that now we have a young lass on the team. She may be a replacement for Sergeant Reed, but it doesn't mean to say she has inherited his bad habits. You and he led us consistently astray in the past, but now is the time to change things. We must not lead her astray and by so not doing we must hope we can haul ourselves back from the brink."

"Rubbish," retorted Berger. "You're only out here because there was nobody like the Chief or myself around to pay for the booze."

"That's slander."

"I'll put it right by saying that though you wouldn't get a round in yourself, you're too much of a something-or-other to ask a girl to buy you a pint."

"By something-or-other, would you mean gentleman?"

"Yes, I would. I've heard it said a gentleman never inflicts pain and I can say from long experience that you never inflict pain—especially on your own wallet."

Green put his paper down and got to his feet. "In that case, son, you won't be disappointed if I leave you out of the first round."

Berger clapped a hand to his head. "Oh, no, what have I done?"

Green ignored him and said to the approaching waiter: "Just put them down here, son."

Four drip mats and four drinks were put on the low table.

Tip said: "The DCI ordered them to be brought for us the moment you came through the door. The bar is a bit crowded because there's a conference on, so we thought it would be better out here."

"I've boobed again," wailed Berger.

"No you haven't son," comforted Green. "You can pay for these drinks at the same time as you order—and pay for—the next round."

Masters who had been examining the luxury gifts in glass cases near the reception desk joined them. "Any luck, Bill?"

"About five minutes after we got into position to keep an eye on the house, her ladyship arrived in a taxi. Within about ten minutes of her coming a car drew up and a very tall chap got out and went indoors. I took him for Kempe, because he had a key to the front door and we have been told he is a biggish chap."

"Then what?"

Tip said, "They were in the house together for nearly forty minutes, Chief. Then they came out together. She had a small carton with her." She turned to Green. "What size was it? About a foot square and half that depth?"

"About that, love."

"They got in the car together and drove back to the restaurant. We followed and saw him drop her there. Then he drove off. She took the carton into the restaurant with her."

Green said, "We couldn't stay there. The car had to be parked where it was before. I got out and kept watch while sugar here did her parking bit. After she rejoined me we continued to keep watch for a bit, but when it seemed obvious that whatever you expected to happen had happened, we packed it in. We didn't look for you, and as you weren't where you were when we left, you could have been anywhere. So we came back here. Arrived best part of an hour ago."

"Thank you. Berger saw her go off in a taxi. . . ."

"As you suspected she would."

"Hoped. I thought she'd get in touch with her husband as soon as we'd left her, but she could have discussed matters on the phone. I was banking on them being too delicate for that and that she'd want to meet him to talk in private. As he was meant to be putting up a marquee, it would have looked odd if he'd turned up at the restaurant and it would look equally odd if she turned up on the camp site. So I guessed at a meeting at home. I hoped I was right."

"As you were." Green lifted his glass. "Cheers! First today."

"Chief," said Tip, putting down her glass of white wine. "What has the meeting between Mr and Mrs Kempe told us?"

"Evidentially or investigationally?"

"Mr Green reported your meeting to me. But it didn't seem to be very conclusive. Nothing to get our teeth into."

"Did you say that to him, or ask him for his views?"

"No, Chief."

"Why not?"

"Because I wanted to work things out for myself, if I could." She wrinkled her brow. "I didn't manage it, not really."

"What does not really mean, love?" asked Green.

"All I could make out of it was that Mrs Kempe seemed very anxious not to incriminate Packard over the hit-and-run business. I mean that's her attitude now. But would that have been her attitude several years ago when her husband was convicted?"

"You tell us, sugar."

"I don't think it would. I think she would have shopped him as leave as look at him, if we can believe all the people we've spoken to."

"Won't do, petal," said Green, shaking his head. "Or rather it will, but the only answer to the question you're asking yourself is that the idea of anybody changing a crumpled wing and other bits and bobs on the damaged car was so fantastic that they never thought of it until far too late. They thought somebody had nicked the car. . . ."

"That couldn't have been right, because of the timings."

"We know, love. But people like the Kempes don't accept the timings in such cases. They think the local police have made a mistake, or, and this is only my theory, mind you . . ."

"What?"

"That Kempe's car was stolen immediately he put it into the garage and before his missus and the other two got to the house. It's a possibility, love. Some joker sees Kempe drive into his garage and come out again without locking up. A nice warm engine to start immediately. Not much noise to be heard. Say Kempe had gone straight to the loo and pulled the chain. He wouldn't have heard the engine, or if he did hear it, he'd think it was his missus and the other two arriving."

"You mean the car could have been back on the same road so quickly that a small error in police timing. . . ."

"Exactly, love. I know there are arguments against it, but that's the way people in the Kempes' situation would think, at any rate for quite a time. And then, I think, they probably began to wonder if two or three people had been involved, just as Annabel said this morning. To ordinary drivers, changing a wing and mending bumpers and lights is unthinkable on their own."

"So you think that by the time they and their friends had, together, got round to the point of suspecting Packard, it was too late for Alan Kempe?"

"That's right, honeybun. He was already in chokey and the evidence about nuts and bolts had been destroyed or rusted or something."

"I see." Tip got to her feet. "Same again everybody?"

"Stay where you are, Tip," said Masters. "I'll get them."

"No, Chief." She grinned. "I don't want to get a name—like the DCI—for not standing my corner."

"You can buy a drink in a moment if you want to. Sit down and listen, please. You made an observation a minute or two ago I want to congratulate you for. You mentioned Mrs Kempe's attitude now and asked whether it would have been the same several years ago. That was exactly the right question to ask. Why?"

"Because you have said we should proceed by playing the old game of spot the difference between then and now."

"And?"

"Even if you hadn't declared your intention of playing it that way, her response to your questioning is curious. Why not mention Packard if he was the suspected villain years ago? Answer, because she now wishes to disassociate herself from him and also to suggest that she never thought him guilty."

"Conclusions?"

"She knows that to mention his name now would associate her with him in our minds, and to suggest that she thought him guilty of shopping her husband would provide us with a motive. She obviously wants to avoid both conclusions occurring to us. Why does she want to do that? Because she is aware something has happened to him. And for her to be aware of that means . . . well it means she's at least seen or heard of him during the last six months."

"Brilliant," said Masters.

"And for that, girlie, you can bring me not only a drink, but a bowl of nuts off the bar as well," said Green.

When Tip had left them, Berger said: "I can never remember you catechizing me quite so closely when I first joined you, Chief."

"Because there was no need. The DCI had worked with you, and you were a man joining men. Tip is well up to standard, but she can't believe she will make the grade."

"Lack of confidence, Chief?"

"She's overcoming that quite quickly. Her trouble is that she won't appreciate that she is only a fledgling sergeant as well as a fledgling in a murder firm. Nobody expects her to be able to fly as far and fast as the rest of us for a while, but she feels she has to. So we all have to encourage her, and by encourage I mean point out mistakes as well as commending her when she does well. And above all, teach her how to think the way people in our job have to."

"Here she is, Chief."

Green looked up. "What kept you, love?"

"They had to refill the nut bowl."

"After grilled Dover sole and side-saddle," said Green, "I could do with a snooze."

"Your side salad, or saddle or whatever you call it," snorted Berger, "consisted of a little lettuce, tomato and cucumber with about a quarter of a stone of sautéed new potatoes. No wonder you're feeling like zizz."

"It's the heat," said Green. "Very soporific, these long, hot, summer days."

"In that case you should have foregone the biscuits and that cut of Stilton you had with them."

Green turned to Tip. "Don't ever grow like the lad here, love, and revile the aged."

Tip looked serious. "I'm going to support him all the way. You shouldn't eat so much in the middle of the day. It's not good for you. Just a little sardine salad would have been enough for lunch. I mean it. I think you should cut down drastically on your eating."

Green looked at her closely, as if unable to believe his ears.

"There's no point in looking at me like that. I'm going to suggest to the Chief that we cut out lunches altogether in this hot weather. After all, he's a very big man and he only had a plate of cold Vichyssoise and a slice of Melba toast."

Green put his hand on her arm. "You know that little sling bag you always carry?"

"Yes."

"Make sure you always carry a couple of Mars bars in

it, petal. Just in case I feel like a snack between meals."

There were almost tears in Tip's voice as she shook her head and said: "You're so silly for such a nice man."

Masters came down the main staircase to join them.

"Conference," he said. "I suppose you could do with a snooze in the shade, Bill, so we'll go along to your bench in the park to talk." He glanced at Berger. "If you and Tip would go on ahead and reserve a seat for us, we'll follow on."

Masters and Green strolled gently towards the lawn dominated by the huge cypress. Green said: "That little lass is trying to mother me."

"Daughter you, don't you mean?"

"Whatever. She's a nice lass. I hope she lives up to your expectations for her."

"She will," confidently asserted Masters. "If she doesn't it will be our fault."

"For not doing what, exactly?"

"I am sure she is intelligent enough to make the grade and to progress normally." Green grunted his assent. Masters went on. "But her intelligence and her abilities have to be channelled towards making her an investigator. All sorts of things have to be built in, like constant suspicion, an awareness of the possibilities of the improbable connections between facts . . . you know the score so I don't have to go on. But while she is assimilating what she must have, she will make mistakes which have to be pointed out and will do good work which must be commended. This sort of treatment affects young people different ways. If we don't play our part carefully, you may find that once she knows her stuff Tip will want to leave us."

"Why, exactly?"

"To start afresh in a different team to which she will go not as a raw beginner, but as a member fully trained to play her part. Where she will not be regarded as a perpetual rookie and every mistake and embarrassment will not be remembered."

"She'd be happier with a fresh start where she can

operate on even terms with anybody of her rank. I can understand that. So how can we make sure we'll keep her if she wants to go, except by blocking any application for transfer she might make?"

"There's only one way, Bill, and that is to make sure she is happy working with us. I don't mean we should overlook her mistakes, I mean she should be happy with us as people. Fortunately she seems to be moderately so with Berger and myself at the moment."

"But not with me?" growled Green.

Masters turned to him and grinned: "I don't for the life of me know why, but for some reason or another she thinks you are the greatest thing since Winston Churchill in his heyday."

"Oh, yeah?"

"That is why she is daughtering you. Sorry about it, Bill, but you'll have to put up with a bit of female smothering."

Green looked highly pleased. "Do you know, George, I don't think I shall mind at all."

"I didn't think you would. And I'm sure you'll treat her in exactly the right way."

"As a father, you mean?"

"Exactly."

They continued in silence until they reached the seat in the sun that Berger had reserved for them. "Here you are, Chief, this is where the DCI spent an hour or so yesterday watching all the girls go by. To overhear us, anybody would have to crash through the bushes and trees behind."

"Excellent, thank you. Where's Tip?"

"Didn't you pass her?"

"No."

"She must have taken a different route. She scooted back to the car to bring an inflatable cushion she put in the boot."

"Whatever for?"

"She thought it would be more comfortable for the DCI to sit on."

155

Masters smothered a grin. "How very thoughtful of her."

Masters and Green sat on the seat. To make it more of a confidential circle, the two sergeants squatted on the grass at their feet.

"George," said Green. when they were all settled, "by guessing Annabel Kempe would want to talk to her old man as soon as possible after we had visited her, it struck me you were definitely tying the Kempes in with Packard's disappearance."

"Quite right. Or, rather, I was testing that theory. Had she not shot off as she did, or even if, unknown to us, she had discussed the matter with her husband over the phone, we should now be none the wiser."

"You'll not accept that there could be an innocent reason for her going off home and for her husband to meet her there?" asked Tip.

"Of course I'll accept that. But I calculate that the chances of that happening are a million to one against. If she had gone back to the house to fetch something she had forgotten, like the parcel you saw her carrying, I'd find that perfectly natural, if a little out of character for somebody who is obviously a very able business person. But for her to call her husband away from an important job to meet her. . . ."

"But that could have been coincidence, Chief."

"Not it, petal," grunted Green. "Not straight after we'd talked to her."

"And considering the subject of our talk," added Masters.

Tip said: "I follow all that. But it offers no actual evidence for going so far as to assume they were involved in Packard's disappearance."

"No hard evidence," agreed Masters, "but enough indications to bolster a theory we already have."

Tip nodded her head to show she had got the point, and Berger was about to speak when he suddenly decided to hold his tongue. Masters looked up to see the reason and noticed a park-keeper coming their way and likely to pass very close. He was a middle-aged man in dark uniform trousers, shirt sleeves and peaked cap. He was obviously doing his rounds and, though nominally just slowly walking the path, he was peering about and bending to look under bushes, presumably looking for damage or caches of rubbish. Quite close to them he stepped on the verge, and with a pair of secateurs cut off a small broken branch from a bush. This he cut into smaller pieces which he pushed into a nearby waste-bin.

He pocketed his secateurs and nodded as he drew level with them. "A very nice park you have here," said Masters.

"No' bard, izzit," agreed the park-keeper in a broad Suffolk accent.

He looked hot and seemed inclined to stop for a chat. Seeing this, Green asked: "Like a fag, chum?"

"Thanks bor." He sat down next to Masters after accepting a light. "Miles of paths in here, you know. Takes some hoofing on a hot day like this."

"Do you get much damage?" asked Masters.

"None to speak on. Bits broken off sometimes. Flower beds don't get vandalized, thank God. 'Course we patrol all the time."

"What is your job? Are you just a keeper or a gardener or what?"

"Bit of everything actually. Keeper and gardener's labourer you might say. I has to dig beds over and such for the gardeners to plant from the glasshouses."

"Do you like it?" asked Tip.

"Aye, I do that. It's a bit cold in winter sometimes. We got a lot of easterly wind across here, you know. Cold enough to freeze an Eskimo's mitten, if you know what I mean, but there's no need to patrol then. Not many people walk in the park in easterlies, not if they're sensible. Then we get on with inside work. The glasshouses are heated, you see, so we do the pricking out and weed the trays. An' we have to spray the houses against pests and mildew, you know, and put a bit o' limewash on. Aye, it's all go. Then early on, when the weather gets a bit better, there'll be railings to paint and fences to mend. And in autumn . . ." He pushed his cap back on his head. "Can you imagine the heaps of leaves we 'as to rake up from this lot?"

"I can imagine," said Masters. "All go for compost, I suppose?"

"Leaf mould, aye. But we 'as to burn some. Fat too many to handle otherwise."

"Tell me," said Masters, changing the subject somewhat, "what you do about this modern idea of leaving areas completely uncultivated and natural as a habitat for butterflies, bees and other wild life? Your park is very natural, but it is very carefully tended, planted and trimmed. I don't think anybody would find a weedy plant anywhere."

"We take care o' that, bor," said the keeper. "Park Superintendent's very keen on it besides him not wanting those environists biting 'is ear. You're not one o' them, are you?"

"No, no. It's just that everything looks so very spick and span and I've not noticed an uncultivated area."

"You want to see one, bor, you wander on down to the lakes. You'll see two there. The islands. We leave them to naturalize. Leave them to the ducks, you might say, an' whatever else wants to breed there. There's trees an' bushes an' grass an' dandelions an' anything else you can think of on them islands."

"How very clever to use them in that way. It means that the animals can have not only food but complete sanctuary there."

" 'Sright, bor. No visitors can get at 'em to catch 'em or trample about standing on nests an' squashing the plants. Kills two birds wi' one stone you might say, bor. Helps the wild life an' us. We doesn't 'ave to go on those islands an' do anything more'n once a year in the autumn. Come October we goes across wi' a pair o' loppers to trim the whins an' brambles. I usually manage to find

158

a pint o' late whortleberries when we go over. Any 'ow, thanks for the chat, gents, an' the fag. I'll have to get on an' make sure nobody's pinched old Ollie's statue."

They watched him disappear round a bend in the path.

"Who the hell is Ollie?" demanded Green.

"Cromwell," said Tip. "I think he's on that solitary statue in the middle of the very big lawn right at the bottom."

Green sucked his partial denture before turning to Masters. "I've not been down there and seen these lakes and islands," he said mildly. "Before we proceed any further, tell me why."

Tip looked from Green to Masters, who did not reply immediately. Then she said in a bewildered little voice, "It was because the day was too hot for you to go down there and climb back again."

Green gazed down at her for a moment, as though he had not heard her. "Not that, love. I want to know why His Nibs has not mentioned before now the fact that he thinks Packard's body is on one of those islands."

"He what?" asked Berger.

"He can't think that," said an astounded Tip.

"I do, actually," said Masters.

"What are we waiting for?" asked Berger, starting to get to his feet.

"Sunset, lad. We can't go barging through jungle undergrowth looking for corpses with all these women and kids around. We'll have to wait till the gates shut and get Harold Knight along here."

"Chief," wailed Tip. "I don't understand. I can't see how. . . ."

"Don't worry, petal. His Nibs is good at bedtime stories and he's going to tell you one now." Green fished out his battered cigarette packet. There was just one in it. "I hope you brought some more of these along, lass. I'll need some more before I've time to get to the shops."

"In the car," said Tip.

Green grunted his dismay at this answer and raised

his eyebrows at Berger. "Don't worry," the sergeant replied to the unspoken question, "I've got a few left."

"Good." Green turned to Masters. "Now, if it's not too much trouble, do you think you could explain why you think Packard lies somewhere on one of those islands?"

"With pleasure," said Masters. "After all, it's what I brought us all out here for."

"I know. And you just engaged that poor, unsuspecting old park-keeper in conversation to drag out of him information to confirm your theory. Areas left to naturalize, indeed! All you wanted to know was whether there was any bit of this park that the gardeners never visited."

"Partly right," admitted Masters. "I was equally interested in the fact that dogs are confined to a fenced off area up at the top end. My theory would have fallen down if dogs were allowed to roam anywhere they liked. Dogs have a nasty habit of nosing through undergrowth and . . ." He stopped in mid-sentence and looked across the lawn, past the giant cedar. The park-keeper had followed the path round this particular enclave and was now visible, fifty or sixty yards away. Masters got to his feet. "Excuse me for a moment. I want another word with our friend over there."

Masters strode across the grass at speed, taking an angle to cut off his quarry.

"Now what?" asked Berger.

Green closed his eyes and leant back. "Wake me up when he condescends to return, will you?"

"The cigarette you are holding will sting you back to life a long time before then," said Tip. She looked at Berger. "Can't you tell me what is going on?"

"All I can tell you is that when the Chief and I walked back through the park this morning he suddenly went all quiet on me. He looked so grim I asked him if he felt all right. I might have known . . . ah, he's had his word with the keeper. He's on the way back."

As Masters sat down again, Green said: "Right, let's have it."

160

"It was when we were talking about dogs sniffing out bodies," said Masters. "The thought came to me that there could have been a very noticeable niffle round the lakes if there had been a dead body lying there."

"And?"

"I asked him if they ever got smells from the lakes in dry weather. He said it always happened when there was a drought period. Some mud would be exposed, and rotting weeds. There was a bit of a smell there, for a time at the end of last year, but only because the water level was low."

"Rubbish," grunted Green. "By the autumn and winter the ponds would be full."

"That's what I thought," agreed Masters.

"More confirmation of your theory?"

"I like to think so. If the park-keepers noticed a smell then, they might have mistaken it for rotting vegetation, but I don't think that was the cause."

"OK," said Green. "Point one to support your theory. Point two, I suppose, is that no dogs and no members of the public can get to the islands and discover a body. Point three is that the gardeners go in there to thin out some of the undergrowth in October, and Packard disappeared in November, so he could have been there, lying hidden among the bushes, ever since then without anybody being any the wiser."

Masters nodded.

"There's just one drawback to all this, Chief," objected Tip. "It holds water if Packard is actually there. But how can you possibly point to a small area like those islands and even suggest that, out of all the thousands of square miles of countryside there are in East Anglia, he could be there?" She frowned in amazement. "We don't even know for sure he is in East Anglia."

"His car's in East Anglia," said Berger, "and where his car is, there will the rep be also."

"Axioms don't count. We only came to Ipswich because the Kempes live here and the Chief wanted to talk to them about that hit-and-run case."

"Not entirely," said Berger. "You yourself found he'd bought a house within spitting distance of Ipswich. All these things add up, you know, to a pretty strong indication of his whereabouts."

"Not a strong enough indication for even somebody like the Chief, who's got a name up for coming to correct conclusions with hardly any data to go on, to calmly sit here and point a finger down that path and say, 'Packard's body is lying over there in some bushes.'" She appealed to Green. "Is there?"

"Is there what, sugar?"

Tip expired in exasperation. "Is there enough evidence for the Chief to say Packard is on one of those islands?"

"Not on one of them, lass," replied Green. "He'll tell you which one. And so will I, and I've never seen them. The one with the little six- or seven-foot-wide canal round half of it."

"That's the first one you come to going from here."

"Is it?"

"Why that one?"

"Because a little cutting that wide and only a couple of feet deep is easier to cross carrying a body than a dirty great expanse of water probably two or three times that depth."

"Give it up," counselled Berger. "Let's hear what the Chief has to say."

"I like to know what's going on. To work it out for myself."

"Have a heart. You've heard and seen everything any of the rest of us has. I certainly don't know how the Chief decided Packard must be on that island, but everything he's said about it being an ideal place of concealment adds up, doesn't it? And the DCI was able to fall into step as soon as the Chief started pointing him that way, and he's not one for swallowing a lot of old hogwash without objecting."

Masters and Green exchanged amused glances.

"Better put the lass out of her misery, George."

"Right you are," agreed Masters. "Facts and support-ing hints in any old order. We've heard the DCI select the island for us—with reasons. He might have added that our information is that Kempe is a very big man. A big man would find it comparatively easy—or easier than a smaller man—to carry a body across what we have heard described as a small, shallow canal."

"So you are saying Kempe killed him, Chief?"

"No, Tip. I haven't said that at all. I merely said he carried Packard's body to the island."

Tip shook her head in bewilderment.

Masters continued. "Obviously the dead body could not be deposited by day. Even in November this park will have a fair sprinkling of people about, and others, like our friend the keeper, will be keeping their eyes open.

"But the gates are closed at sunset, so getting the body into the park itself would be difficult, and without the possibility of getting a car in, transporting it would be next to impossible, for though a big man like Kempe could carry a body six or seven feet across shallow water, carrying the same body across the distances imposed by this park would make Atlas wince."

"So you've shot down your own theory, Chief."

"Not quite, Tip. I wanted to raise the difficulties with you, just as I had to raise them in my own mind before I could overcome them." He looked at her. "You have a street map in your bag."

"Yes, Chief."

"With the Kempes' house and restaurant both marked on it?"

"Not the buildings themselves, Chief, just the streets in which they are located, because I didn't know where-abouts in the streets they were."

"Hand your map to the DCI, please."

As Tip opened her shoulder bag to take out the folded street plan, Masters asked Green: "Have you studied the map, Bill?"

"No, I saw it in the girlie's hand, of course, but I didn't think there was any need for the services of the firm's map-reading buff just to find our way from A to B."

"Take a look now, please."

Tip handed the open sheet over, and Green took his time. He sat sideways on the bench and spread the map out beside him. At last he looked up. "The Capercaillie is nowhere near the park. By that I mean it's a quarter of a mile from the main entrance and, as you know, surrounded by all manner of streets and alleys, but with no covered or easy approach to the gates. However, the house is a different kettle of fish.

"The street where the Kempes live has been marked here, by Tip, with a very little neat red cross. At the beginning of the printed street name—Chanctonbury Road—and a very long street. Where we entered it, near the red mark close to the C of Chanctonbury, we were a long way from the park. Over half a mile actually, and that's a long way in this town. So you don't realize that at one point the road gets quite close to the park, and that it is fairly near where I estimate the Kempes' house to be. But that's not the point. If you look carefully at the plan you will see another of those eight-foot-wide approaches to the park gates. Exactly like the one we use to get in at the north-western end when we come here on foot from The Blenheim. Only this one is much shorter, and it is pretty close to the Kempe house." He looked up. "More important, it enters in the northern half of the eastern side where the two paths join."

"Why do the points of the compass make it more important?" asked Berger.

Green stood up, and moved a few yards away from the bench until he had a view through the trees to the steep grassy slopes of the hill. He pointed directly at the summit. "That," he said, "is the northern half of the eastern side of the park."

Berger and Tip stood by Green's side and followed the direction of his finger. Berger started to whistle through his teeth. Tip looked from one to the other in bewilderment.

"Rolled him down?" Berger asked Green, quietly.

164

"I don't see why not. Of course a body wouldn't go all the way down, or I don't think it would. But if that grass is as smooth and short as it looks from here. . . ."

"Which it is," said Berger.

"How do you know?" asked Tip. "You've not been over there."

"They were grazing a flock of sheep on it yesterday. Sheep nibble it short."

"Oh, yes. I remember seeing them."

"Well, as I was saying," continued Green, "on that sort of surface and that sort of incline a good shove would roll a body down a few yards each time."

"That's horrible," said Tip.

"Not as horrible as seeing him off in the first place," grunted Green. "But if you're going to bilk at the body being rolled down, let me point out to you that carrying it down pick-a-back would be a damn sight easier than carrying it up or even on the level. And, for a bet, that slope runs right down to the bed of that tiny rivulet you told me about. The one that feeds the pond we want."

"It does," said Berger, "and even after the slope reaches the stream it's still down-hill for the last twenty or thirty yards to the island."

White-faced, Tip returned to her seat on the grass near Masters, who had been able to overhear all that had gone on. He had taken the opportunity to fill his pipe and was now sending up a cloud of Warlock Flake smoke. "Keeps the flies away," he said. "There's quite a plague of Little Men of Wroot round here."

"Little what?" she asked quietly.

"Little Men of Wroot. See, here's one." He picked up from the bench a very small, slender, black insect with a little red mark on its wing casings and showed it to her. "They don't bite, only tickle. I was on Nottingham station once, in the early evening in weather such as this. It was when there were still a few steam trains about. The train before the one I wanted was pretty crowded and the engine couldn't pull it away. There was a plague of these little chaps at the time and so many of their bodies had got squashed on the line that the wheels couldn't get enough grip. They had to bring up a second locomotive and couple them in tandem to get enough power to draw away."

"It was like that down at Brighton in seventy-six," said Green, who had rejoined them. "I took my missus down there and as we walked along the prom we just crushed ladybirds in the thousands. But for these little jiggers," said Green, waving his hands in front of his face to clear them away, "you want a flock of starlings. They just swoop around with their mouths open and shovel them up by the beakful."

"Chief."

Masters looked at her strained white face. "Yes, Tip?"

"It's awfully nice of you and Mr Green to try and take my mind off things by talking all this nonsense about Little Men of Wroot—which I don't believe is the right name for them anyway—but you've just solved a murder and there's this ghastly idea of rolling a dead man down that great hill."

"We haven't solved a murder, Tip. We've only just begun. And it's our job. Yours, too, now. You can't expect us to get solemn about doing our job successfully, can you?"

"No, I suppose not."

"I tell you what. Why don't you and Sergeant Berger get out of this plague of . . . er . . . Little Men of Wroot by going for the car. Mr Green and I will walk down to the main gates and you can meet us there. And while you are getting the car out on to the road, Berger can ring the local nick and ask DCI Knight if I can call on him straight away."

"Right, Chief," said Berger.

"Stress the urgency, please."

7

The two pairs went in opposite directions. Masters deliberately led Green by smaller side paths along a route which soon brought them out of the western area of lawns, flower beds and copses. As they stepped out into the open and the broad expanse of downland before them, Green stopped to gaze about him.

"I'd seen the hill, of course, from the northwest gate. But I didn't get this view of it. There's acres of country here, George."

"Has that any significance, Bill?"

"I think so. On a winter's night, which was when we think the Kempes brought Packard's body into the park, they would be able to see more easily than if they'd had to pass through trees. The whole of that slope could have been bathed in moonlight, which would have made it as bright as day or, if there wasn't a moon to speak of, even ordinary starlight or the luminescence from clouds would have been enough for them. No shadows from trees or buildings, you see, George. And probably more important, no great surrounding splodges of artificial light to spoil night vision."

"So you still think our theory holds?"

"More than ever. In spite of what young Tip thinks, I'm pretty sure they'd roll the body down. Macabre to think of, I know. But if I'd been faced with the same problem, that's what I'd have done. It would take ten minutes at least, but it would be a damn sight easier than carrying a body all that way."

They began to move along the path that ran down the

re-entrant towards the lake. "I'm pleased to have your confirmation—more or less—of what I thought myself, Bill."

"And what was that?"

"I thought that they might have used some sort of tarpaulin or groundsheet and pulled it down the hill with the body on it."

Green thought for a moment. "It's a good suggestion, George."

"I thought of it, I suppose, because it's a trick I use myself on occasion. Do you remember when I had to move the freezer out of the kitchen when I was decorating?"

"Yes."

"I tilted it until I could ease a piece of carpet underneath—big enough to leave me with a decent handhold—and I was able to drag it very easily, even over a level floor. A weight I couldn't have lifted otherwise. I do the same thing when Wanda wants me to move the big wardrobe in our bedroom so that she can clean behind it. So if I can do that with tall heavy items, I reckoned Kempe would be able to do it very easily with a body, moving down a hill like that."

"I like it," said Green. "I'll put your idea to the lassie— it'll probably make her feel better. And by the way, George, what about her reaction? Can we wear that every time a body is mentioned, let alone seen? Bearing in mind this is her first case, of course."

"Have you ever got over your sensitivity when faced with a murdered body, Bill?"

Green sucked his teeth. "Some affect me more than others, of course. Kids and young girls mutilated, old 'uns done in brutally . . . no, I've never got over it. I've learned not to show it too much, I suppose, but my guts still turn over on some of our jobs."

"That about describes my feelings. I get a momentary twinge no matter who it is, and the twinge leaves a nasty feeling for a long time after. I should be very worried about Tip if I thought she had no sensitivity."

"Me, too. I was hoping you'd see it that way. Just so long as her feelings don't hamper proceedings."

"She was using her imagination, just now, Bill. Seeing things in her mind's eye which would revolt any normal young woman. And we need her to have imagination, don't we? She'd be of no use to us if she was solid ivory from the neck up."

Green grunted his agreement. "This the little rivulet, George?"

"That's it. Pretty, isn't it? Just purling down the slope at no more than a cupful a second."

"It will spate in wet weather. Then you'd get a bucketful a second. If I were a kid, I'd be dropping matchsticks in there to watch them travel down."

"It's a pity the job we're on isn't quite as innocent."

Green didn't reply. The lake and its island were now so close as to claim all his interest. They stopped as they came to the railing separating the path from the narrow canal between the island and the bank. They leaned on the top rail.

"Seven feet wide," guessed Green. "And only six or eight inches deep. A squidgy bottom, I'd say. Mud and dead vegetation." He looked round at Masters. "It's a foot or fourteen inches below the height of this bank, so even if it was full to overflowing last November, which I can't think it was, it would be very easy to cross on foot, with or without a heavy burden."

"Two feet overall at most?"

"Allowing for sinking into the ooze a bit, yes. Easily done in a pair of gum boots."

"And the island? You can guess its size from here. Big enough for hiding a body?"

"I could hide two platoons of light infantry in there," declared Green. "There are one or two clear patches where the ducks and geese are roosting, but the rest of it is made for concealment."

Masters straightened up. "We'd better get on. The car will be there by now, I imagine, and I don't want to keep Harold Knight waiting."

As they moved away, Green said: "You never told me what that thought was that had you guessing a day or two ago. You said the sight of Harry Moller had called not only it back to you, but something else as well."

"Ah, yes. I had intended to discuss those ideas with you in private, so now is as good a time as any. They won't take long and we have a few minutes' walk ahead of us."

"I'm listening."

Masters spoke very briefly, mentioning the two points that had occurred to him. Green heard him out and then said: "They're both useful ideas, George. In fact they could be the key to this business. Do I take it that you have accepted both and have used them in arriving at the theory that Packard is on that island?"

"Yes. I worked it out, and I couldn't for the life of me see where he could be, other than there."

"Unless he'd been buried in some spot we'd never discover? Up near his house, probably?"

"That was the alternative. And we're just not equipped to cope with that, so I had no other course open to me than to go for the island theory."

"You could have thrown your hand in."

"As a last resort, yes. I have considered going back to Anderson, giving him the story and letting him arrange for East Anglia to be dug over. But it's no use doing that until we're beaten, so I've decided to have that island searched."

"It gels," grunted Green. "He'll be there."

"I think I can see the two sergeants eating ice-creams at the kiosk."

"Why not? I think I'll have one myself."

When the two sergeants left Masters and Green to return to The Blenheim for the car, Berger waited until they were out of earshot and then said: "Can I give you a bit of advice?"

"Why not?" said Tip. "I seem to be getting it from all sides at the moment. What have I done wrong now?"

"Don't get shirty. I was only going to say that you can feel what you like about corpses and their treatment."

"Thanks."

"But don't use those feelings to make it sound as though you were accusing the Chief and the DCI, and me, too, for that matter, of not giving two hoots in hell as to what goes on in the job. The Chief, Bill Green and I all have our sensibilities, if that's the right word. We don't like corpses, murders and so on any more than anybody else. But in our particular job you have to learn to cope with your feelings, otherwise you'd have to cop out. And when I say cope with them, I don't mean suppress them altogether. I mean deal with them privately and don't get all het up and bother other people with them. They've got their own to deal with and that's a hard enough job on its own."

"I'm sorry," said Tip quietly. "But I couldn't get out of my head that body rolling down the hill, with its arms flailing and . . ."

Berger looked down at her and then fished in his pocket. He handed the unfolded handkerchief to her. She accepted it in silence.

Tip had obviously recovered her composure by the time Masters and Green joined them at the gate.

"You've got a blob of ice-cream on your chin, petal," said Green.

Tip rubbed her hand across it and looked at her palm. "Where's the ice-cream?" she demanded.

"Over there," said Green, pointing towards the kiosk. "His Nibs and I will have a slider apiece while we sit on this bench here." He handed her a pound coin. "You and the lad won't want another, so that'll cover it."

"And I asked to join a murder firm, just to queue among children at an ice-cream stall!"

"We all have to start somewhere, sugar," said Green airily. "Make them both vanilla, there's a love."

"Ice-cream!" muttered Tip again.

"That's right, petal," said Green quietly in her ear. "We

171

have to do everything we can to keep cool in this job."

Berger was talking to Masters. "DCI Knight is expecting to be in his office all afternoon, Chief. He says you can go along to see him as soon as you like."

"Thank you. Did he ask why I want to talk to him?"

"Not in so many words, Chief. He asked how we were getting on and I told him I thought you had made some progress, but I didn't specify anything."

"Good. I obviously don't want to say too much, but we have to have his co-operation over searching the island. We have no authority with the park staff."

"He promised you his full co-operation, Chief."

"But not blind co-operation."

As they ate the ice-creams, Green said: "I've been telling honeybun here of your idea about the body being dragged down on a tarpaulin, George. She tells me it could best be done on a good long length of old stair carpet out of the loft. That's if Kempe has a good long length of old stair carpet in his loft."

Masters accepted this idea gravely. "I must agree that the longer the piece of material under the body, the better the handhold would be, the more upright the puller could be and—though mechanics are not my strong point—the expenditure of energy in foot/pounds, I believe, would be considerably less to achieve the same result."

Tip smiled gratefully for this consideration and took the map to consult it.

"It's no more than a lock of perches from here to the local nick, is it?" Green asked her.

"It's quite close, but I think there's some one way traffic on the most direct route. If we just go on along the way we're facing until we get to Civic Street and then turn left we'll be almost there."

"In that case," said Masters, wiping his hands on his handkerchief, "let's be on our way."

DCI Knight had obviously warned the station sergeant of their expected arrival, and they were shown immediately into his office.

"Hello, sir," he greeted Masters. "I've just had the first reports from the sergeant I sent up to look at Walesby Cottage. He's got a couple of constables with him and I told them to probe every inch of the garden, just in case."

"Ah! I take it they found nothing?"

"In the garden? No. They're both country born and bred and they're prepared to swear nobody has turned a spoonful of that earth over for two or three years. Is that what you expected?"

"Yes."

"You think the cadaver is somewhere else?"

"It's got to be, Harold, hasn't it, if it isn't at the Cottage."

Knight laughed. "Of course. That was a bloody silly remark of mine. What I meant to ask Mr Masters was whether he had any idea where the body might be. I'm assuming there is one, of course."

"We definitely believe Packard is dead," said Masters.

"And the location of the body?"

Masters winced a little at the wording of the question, but answered it readily enough. "We think it is on the island in the larger of the two lakes in Christchurch Park."

If they had expected Knight to show disbelief or surprise or to ask for proof, they were disappointed. He merely said: "In that case the sooner somebody has a look there, the better."

"You'd like to be told why we think it is there before taking any action?"

"No, sir. If a child of six walked in here and told me he thought there was the body of a dead man on that island I'd be bound to go there and look, just in case the kid was right. If Detective Chief Superintendent George Masters walks in here and tells me he thinks there's a corpse on the island. . . ." He shrugged. "Of course I'd appreciate hearing the reasons for your belief, sir, but if you prefer it they can wait until we've proved whether you're right or wrong."

"That is very generous of you."

Knight grinned and shook his head. "Yesterday a secret cottage and a missing car. Today a dead body. What's it going to be tomorrow? I can hardly wait to hear. Meanwhile, if you'll give me a couple of minutes on the phone to the Parks Superintendent, I'll get permission for two of us to wade across to the island. I don't think we want to make too much of a thing of it to begin with."

"I agree. No sirens and ambulances and no hint of closing the park. Just a couple of plain clothes men in waders slipping across the rail as if they were park employees on some job."

"Right. Shall you go yourself, sir?"

"I think not. Perhaps Sergeant Berger in his shirt sleeves and one of your constables dressed not too reputably . . ."

"Good. We'll stand on the bye lines." He picked up the phone. "I'll not mention we're looking for a body, just that we've been told the proceeds of a crime have been stashed away there and we'd like a quick look."

"Excellent."

Within a quarter of an hour they were returning towards the park gates. When they arrived, Berger and Detective Constable Stewart, each carrying a pair of thigh boots, went on ahead. Green and Tip followed, with Masters and Knight bringing up the rear.

The railings were waist high for a man. Berger and Stewart climbed over easily enough. Green stood leaning back on the railing, Tip leant forward on it, looking at the ducks and conversing like any normal couple. Masters and Knight chose to sit on the grass on the other side of the path, far enough away from the others to avoid giving the appearance of a crowd. Masters took the opportunity to give Knight a fairly full account of his reasons for selecting the island as the likeliest spot for Packard's corpse to have been hidden.

"No hard evidence," said Knight, "but a hell of a lot of the old circumstantial, sir. Let's keep our fingers crossed. Those lads have been over there for the best part of ten minutes now."

"I told Berger to search extremely carefully. Not that he needed telling, of course, but at times like this I'm like an old hen with her chicks."

"You are, sir? I'd never have thought that."

"Internal tremors," confessed Masters. "Getting worse with every minute that passes and . . ."

"Save it, sir? There's your sergeant, and he's signalling to Mr Green. Thumbs up, I think."

"I think we should stay here," counselled Masters. It took an effort to say it, but he was very loth to attract the attention of visitors to the park and to see a gawping crowd gather.

Green strolled over to them. "Found," he said quietly.

"Packard?"

"No information yet, but who else?"

Green turned away to rejoin Tip.

"Now what?" asked Knight quietly.

"Another hour or two won't matter. I think you should lay on the whole shooting match for ten minutes after the gates close. There'll be complete privacy, because nobody from outside can see the lake."

"Light?"

"There should still be plenty at sundown, but perhaps you could cajole the management into shutting the gates half an hour early. How do they clear the place, anyway?"

"Haven't a clue," confessed Knight. "I suppose the keepers walk the paths. They probably have a bell to sound half-an-hour before closing time."

"I'll leave it to you, Harold. But I think we ought to have a plain clothes man on inconspicuous duty until we get in your circus."

"What about you, sir?"

"All I want to know is if the body can be positively identified as Packard. If so, how he died. Your forensic people ought to be able to give me that fairly quickly."

"Any guesses?"

Masters looked at him. "Guesses?"

"Calculated ones, sir?"

"Yes. There will be no broken bones."

175

Knight stared at him. "No blunt instruments, traffic accident, shooting?"

"I think not." Masters got to his feet as Berger approached. The sergeant had taken off his thigh boots and was now dressed as he normally was.

"Only a skeleton, Chief, but it's Packard's. It's got that presentation watch round the left wrist. Not much clothing left, but enough for identification purposes. As soon as I made sure of the watch I came out. Constable Stewart is on watch."

"Thank you, Sergeant," said Masters. He turned to Knight. "You heard all that?"

"Yes, sir."

"If you will let me know the arrangements for this evening, I can now leave it to you."

"It's your case, sir."

"True, but it's your body. I shall continue with the case, but I haven't got the means for dealing with the body. It has to be your S of C boys, forensics, photographers and so on who deal with the remains. My only interest is in hearing from you what the cause of death was. But I shall be here with my people at the time you start to operate, just in case we can be of help."

Knight grimaced. "You're right, of course, sir. I'll arrange everything and inform the coroner. Shall I give you a ring at The Blenheim when I know the times?"

"Better than that, come and tell us the arrangements—over a drink. About half past six if you've got everything teed up by then. That should give you enough time to have a quickie, because I can't see the park being clear much before nine, and once the arrangements have been made, you'll be at a loose end anyway."

Knight accepted the invitation eagerly. "Just one thing, sir. Do you mind if I bring my missus? I've told her about you often enough, and now she knows you're down here. . . ."

"We shall be delighted to meet Mrs Knight. I should have included her in the original invitation."

"No bones broken, sir. I was an off-the-cuff arrangement. So . . . if there's nothing more for the moment. It's nearly four o'clock and there's lots to do."

"What now, Chief?" asked Tip as they walked slowly towards the car.

"Tea, lass," said Green firmly. "Scones, jam, cream. . . ."

"How could you?" demanded Tip. "At a time like this, think of jam and cream?"

"Time like what, love?"

Tip spread her hands. "Well . . . immediately after finding a dead body. . . ."

"Darling," said Green gently, "if we didn't eat every time we were dealing with a dead body we'd all be skeletons ourselves."

In the end, nobody had tea. Tip and Berger went off to fill the car while Masters and Green, conscious of the fact that Harold Knight and his wife would be joining them in a relatively short time, went off to bathe and change.

Masters took his time. He lay in a warm bath for a long time, thinking, and then after getting out and towelling down, he went over to the phone. There, with nothing more than the bath sheet round his middle so that any heat and subsequent moisture caused by the warmth of the bath water could transpire and dry from his body, he rang the AC (Crime).

Masters hated putting a clean shirt on directly after a bath. He always had the feeling that still-moist skin would ruin its crispness and reduce it to a damp compress for the rest of the evening. He felt totally sybaritic as he lay back in one of the armchairs, phone to his ear, to report success.

Anderson came on.

"Masters here, sir. I hoped I'd be able to catch you before you left the office."

"George! I've been hoping to hear from you. Beryl has been making my life a misery, asking for news. I hope you've got something for me to tell her."

"I have some news for you, sir, but whether you'll want to tell Mrs Anderson about it is a different matter."

"Like that is it? You're telling me he's dead?"

"We found his body—skeleton actually—this afternoon."

"Skeleton? Are you sure it is Packard?"

"There is a presentation gold watch on the wrist. It exactly fits the description of one given to Packard by his employers some time ago. And sir, I think I should add that the remains were found exactly where we expected to find them."

"You'd worked it out, you mean?"

"Yes, sir."

"How did he die?"

"I can't tell you that yet, sir. The forensic people won't be able to start their examination till later this evening."

"Could he have died naturally?"

"I think not, sir. The body was concealed on an overgrown island in the middle of a lake in the park here. People who die natural deaths don't often choose places like that in which to do it."

There was a moment of silence. Then—

"George, I don't want to tell Beryl all this until you are one hundred per cent sure. . . ."

"Fair enough, sir. But there is something a little less gruesome you can pass on to Mrs Anderson."

"What's that?"

"We found Packard's car."

"In good order?"

"Yes, sir."

"Where was it?"

"Locked safely away in the garage of a house called Walesby Cottage, not far north of here."

"What was it doing there?"

"The house belonged to Packard, sir. He'd bought it secretly. Unbeknown to his wife at any rate. And, sir, I think I should tell you that he bought it for cash which was, I believe, the accumulated pay-off for quite a number of shady deals over the years."

"Bad hat, was he?"

"I think you could safely say he was, sir."

"I'd better keep all that under my hat for the time being, George. About the shady deals, I mean."

"You must have met Packard at some time, sir. What was your opinion of him?"

"Only met him twice. At weddings. We didn't have enough to do with each other for me to form an opinion. After what you've told me, he probably thought it wise to steer clear of a senior policeman."

"Probably, sir. Anyhow, that's it so far. We shan't let the story break for a bit if we can help it. Word may leak out that a skeleton has been found, of course, but we shall not divulge the identity and facts leading to the discovery, so Mrs Anderson and Mrs Packard won't learn of it from reporters. That leaves you free to say as much or as little as you like."

"Thanks, George. But I must say you've left me in a bit of a quandary."

"I sympathize, sir, but it was Mrs Anderson who twisted our arms in the first place."

"I know, I know. But that doesn't make it any better. Beryl was expecting you to turn up and say you'd found the fellow wandering round the streets of Ashby-de-le-Zouche suffering from loss of memory."

"Sorry, sir."

"Not your fault, George. Oh, by the way, how's that new young woman of yours shaping up?"

"Sergeant Tippen? There's absolutely nothing wrong with her shape as far as I can tell, sir."

"Don't be facetious, George. Is she pulling her weight?"

"She'll do, sir. This has been an unpleasant case for an absolute newcomer, and the discovery of a corpse this afternoon made the thought of eating tea distasteful to her. But I would expect that. I wouldn't want a hard-bitten, insensitive girl on the team."

"You're satisfied with her, then?"

"So far, sir, I am. And it will be my fault if she fails,

because she's got all the makings of a good replacement for Reed."

"Excellent. Keep in touch, George, and get back here as soon as possible."

"Right, sir."

After Anderson, Masters spoke to Wanda. He phoned her at some time every day when he was away from home, but the calls he liked best were those such as this one when he could assure his wife that he was approaching the end of the case and his return to her was imminent.

Shortly after he had put the phone down and was only half dressed there was a knock at the door. Green.

"Come in, Bill. Excuse the state of undress, but I've had a session with Anderson."

"How does his pulse beat?" growled Green, taking one of the two easy chairs in the window. "Pleased we've found his wife's half-cousin twice removed's husband at last?"

Masters shook his head. "He's not looking forward to breaking the news to Beryl."

"I'll bet!" Green lit a cigarette. "What's the form, George?"

"I think it will simply be wait and see as far as we are concerned this evening, Bill. I feel I should be there when the body is brought out, but. . . ."

"You? Meaning you don't want us."

"Meaning there's no need for you and Tip to hang about in the park if you don't want to come. Berger and I can go down to keep a watching brief, because that is all I can see us doing until we have a report from the labs. Incidentally, Bill, are ducks omnivorous?"

"Come again?"

"Are ducks omnivorous? I know they eat vegetable matter and bread and all the rest of the stuff people throw to them, but do they eat meat?"

"Dunno," said Green. "Ask Harry Moller."

"I don't want to involve him when he's on holiday, but I think I shall have to."

"You're wondering about young Berger saying it was just a skeleton left?"

"Yes."

"Why? Six or seven months lying in the open is long enough to do that."

"You're probably right. But it seemed as though his clothes had almost gone, too. I'd have expected them to have lasted a bit longer than that."

Green shrugged. "There's no telling with these things. All manner of conditions affect them. Even the composition of the soil. But you don't need me to tell you that."

Masters knotted his tie carefully. "We've got to try and find the means, Bill. The less of anything there is on that island the harder it's going to be for us."

"Agreed. But there's no point in getting steamed up about it." He switched topics. "It's a pity they don't send round a buckshee sherry *every* night of your stay here. It's a custom I could grow very fond of."

"I must say I found it very gracious—both the giving and the living with a schooner of Amontillado. No wonder Harry Moller brings his wife here quite often."

Masters packed his pockets with the assortment of articles he habitually carried. "All ready, Bill? I want to make sure I'm downstairs to greet Knight and his lady."

Green heaved himself to his feet. "I wonder if she'll be tall and icy? Like the drink I'm looking forward to myself."

It was a pleasant enough interlude of three quarters of an hour or so with Harold and Janice Knight. The couple then left with Masters promising that he would be at the main park gate at eight-thirty.

"Right, you two," said Green to Tip and Berger as soon as their guests had gone. "A quick dinner tonight. No fancy stuff. I want to be away from here in exactly one hour's time." He looked at Tip. "And if you don't fancy doing the Lambeth Walk in those glad-rags, petal, you'll have to give yourself time to change into something more serviceable." He turned to the girl behind the bar. "Be a

181

poppet and ask the manager to whistle up the menus, will you, love? We're in a hurry."

Such was the standard of service at The Blenheim that within five minutes they were sitting in an otherwise deserted dining room making the most of a wondrous cool fruit concoction put down in champagne and served in stemmed glasses the size of soup cups. When required to do so, the head waiter could put his foot down. As a plate was emptied it was whisked away and another took its place until the meal ended with minutes to spare before Green's stated deadline.

While Tip sped off to her room to change into jeans, Masters approached the manager who was standing guard in his foyer, watchful for the needs of his guests who were now beginning to come in larger numbers for dinner or to use the bar.

"I wonder if you would mind telling me something."

"If I can, sir, certainly."

"The Capercaillie restaurant. What is its standard? Professional opinion, please."

"It is very good, sir. Very good indeed, and we recommend it very often to people for whom we cannot cater. But you must understand, sir, that it is something of an oddity in that it is open very early in the morning to provide businessmen with breakfast. Then it provides appropriate meals or refreshments at all times throughout the day including dinner at night, and they do outside catering. Everything about it is good. The service, cleanliness and so on. . . ."

"And the cooking?"

"First class, sir. My wife and children go there from time to time for tea because they provide such very good cakes. I have had dinner there, too, spying on the opposition as it were. I came away impressed."

"I see. So they have a good chef?"

"I understand that Mrs Kempe herself is a first-class confectionery cook, sir, so she is knowledgeable enough to make sure that what is served is of a good standard."

"Thank you."

"Are you proposing to visit The Capercaillie for a meal, Mr Masters?"

"I have no plans to do so. I asked merely because I was told that it was a very good place to use when working in the town."

"So it is, sir. It definitely fulfils a need. As a cricketing man I should describe it as a good all-rounder."

Masters smiled. "And your own restaurant?"

"A good number three, sir. A stroke player of elegance and power with all the shots."

"I can't disagree with you."

Masters joined Green and Berger as Tip came down the stairs. "All set?"

They found Knight waiting for them at the main gate.

"We're not putting them out very much," said the local man, nodding towards the house at the entrance. "Several of the keepers live inside. You've probably noticed their houses? They have to come in and out, of course, so there's nothing out of the ordinary in them opening up for cars after hours."

A minute or two later a small convey of cars and a police ambulance joined them. The gates were opened and they travelled at about fifteen miles an hour to the spot where Berger had originally crossed the railings. DC Stewart was waiting to lead the party to the body.

"Will you want lights?" Knight asked the pathologist, who was pulling on a pair of fisherman's waders.

"I don't think so. I'm not expecting to be able to glean much in there and the natural light is still quite strong. A torch perhaps, for looking under bushes."

After ten minutes or so, camera flashes indicated that photographs were being taken. Knight obviously thought he required very few, for the photographer was soon carrying his equipment back across the canal.

"Oughtn't one of us to be in there, Chief?"

"No, Tip. This part of it is not our job."

"Does that mean you think there is nothing to be

seen that would help us? I mean, would you be in there looking around if you thought there could be anything to help us?"

Masters smiled at her. "I think you've summed it up, Tip."

She surprised him by saying, "I'd like to go over. Can I go as your representative?"

He waited a moment before replying. "Yes, you can go. But only with the intention of looking about you without getting into people's way. As I told you, I don't think there'll be anything for us, but you never know."

"And in any case," added Green, who had overheard the conversation, "it'll not be a bad opportunity to get that twisted feeling out of your guts, will it, petal?"

Tip gave a little smile and a moment or two later, wearing a pair of rubber boots some sizes too large for her, she was crossing to the island.

Half an hour went by and it was twilight before the pathologist returned. "They're bringing it out now," he said to Knight and Masters who stood by while he took off his waders. "Nothing to see there except the skeleton. I can't tell you how he died, Chief Inspector, except to say that none of his bones is broken and he wasn't strangled. Hyoid intact. Trouble is, of course, that there are none of his organs there for testing. Only things I've got are a few bits of clothing from under the body and his shoes, of course."

"Were his shoes still on?" asked Masters.

"More or less."

"Any adipocere where the feet were still encased?"

"I think not. Too dry for that, I'd have said. If they'd been immersed it would have been a different story perhaps."

"So what is your immediate opinion?" asked Knight.

"The obvious answer to that is he was poisoned. But without the organs to play with it's going to be difficult to decide the agent. I've taken soil samples from close by in case he vomited and there are still any traces of the poison left, but I'd advise you not to pin your hopes on my finding anything." He flung the waders into the boot of his car. "It's my guess you're going to have a bit of trouble with this one. So am I, but at least you've been able to tell me how old he is and when you think he died. Every little bit helps." He opened the car door. "And now I suppose you'll want to know when you can have a copy of my report?"

"Yes, please."

"Day after tomorrow. But as I say, if I were you I'd proceed as if you'll get no help from me. If there is anything, it will be a bit of a bonus for you." He got into the car. "I'll be in touch, Chief Inspector."

Berger drove the car back to The Blenheim. Tip sat very quietly alongside him until Green said: "Come on, love, out with it. You didn't like the experience, did you?"

"No, I didn't," the girl confessed, "but I managed it."

"Good for you."

"There was one thing I wanted to ask, Chief."

"What was that, Tip?"

"Do ducks build nests?"

Green turned to Masters. "You asked if they were carnivorous?"

"I did. But to answer Tip's question. I don't know. I confess I have never seen a duck's nest or even heard of one. But I presume they have to lay eggs somewhere. If I thought about it I'd have to say that I thought they laid them on the ground or in the reeds."

"Somewhere watery, in any case," said Green. "Don't forget that ducks' eggs, which make a pretty good meal, have to be hard boiled. The shells are porous, you see, and the fear is that they get wet and various nasties can soak through to inside. Hard boiling kills off any bugs there may be."

"Does that answer your question, Tip?"

"No, Chief, not really. You see I saw snips of material—Packard's clothing, I think—and it looked to me as though . . ."

"As though what, Tip?"

"As though they'd been torn off, after the material had

rotted a bit, by . . . by beaks . . . and used for nests. I mean," she went on hurriedly, "lots of birds do pick up scraps of material and quite large rolls of soft wool out of hedgerows where the sheep have caught on thorns and twigs. They line their nests that way."

"They do, indeed, but I'm not qualified to say whether ducks do that sort of thing or not."

"What you have to remember," said Green, "is that there are lots of different ducks there. And they don't necessarily have the same habits as domestic ducks. Some do things the others don't. There are diving ducks and ducks that whistle, for instance. So there may be some among that lot that play at houses."

"There is another possibility," said Masters as they reached the hotel. "Ducks are not the only birds that use those islands. There may be others there that gather material for their nests."

"What we all need," said Green, "is a snifter."

"I think I'd like a shower first," said Tip.

"You do that, love. We'll line one up for you."

"It'll only take me two or three minutes, Chief," she said apologetically.

"As long as that?" asked Green. "In that case there'll be two lined up for you by the time you get down."

Harry and Celia Moller were sitting at one of the long coffee tables in the foyer. As Masters entered, Moller waved.

"I'll invite them to join us for a drink," said Masters quietly to Green.

"Meaning you want to pick his brains."

"He may know something about the habits of ducks."

"Why not? He's that sort of boffin."

"I'll join you shortly—with or without them."

"Had dinner?" asked Moller after Masters had greeted Celia.

"We were sitting outside the dining room door waiting for it to open."

"Like that?" grinned Moller. "I know from experience

186

what that means. You've been out on the job this evening."

"Quite right. Now we're going to have a drink. Will you and Celia join us?"

"Harry will, I expect," said his wife with a smile. "If you'll excuse me, I think I'll go to bed. We've had a tiring day."

"Sightseeing?"

"Bird-watching," said Moller. "Looking at avocets in the colonies at Minsmere and Havergate Island."

Masters almost held his breath.

"Avocets?" he said quietly. "I see."

"They used to be very plentiful in England," said Celia, "but they nearly died out when fen drainage started a couple of hundred years ago. And they were shot because their feathers made good fishing flies. But after the last war we started to get them back again. Not many pairs, of course, but enough to give us hope that they will re-establish here."

"I see."

"That's why we come to The Blenheim," said Moller. "Not only is it an excellent pub, but it's a pretty good centre for getting to the East Anglian breeding grounds. Celia was keen to see the avocets. They're only summer visitors to the Suffolk breeding sites, so one has to choose one's time here, though some winter in the Tamar estuary in Devon."

Masters, still standing, said: "Are you sure you won't have that drink, Celia?"

Moller looked up at him. "There's something on your mind, George."

"There is. I've begun to take a sudden interest in birds. Ducks mainly. I'd like to know more about them."

"Celia is the buff," replied Moller. "I only come along for the ride, really."

"I'll not join you for a drink if you don't mind, Mr Masters," said Celia. "But if your interest in ducks is still as strong as ever tomorrow. . . ."

"It will be," said Masters gravely.

"In that case, I'll make a point of being here, in this

same seat, immediately after breakfast. I can talk to you then, while Harry does his crossword puzzle."

"Thank you, I look forward to our chat."

Celia got to her feet. "Don't keep Harry up too long, Mr Masters, but do tell him what you are doing down here. I told him to ask you, but he said if you wanted him to know you'd tell him. So I've asked on his behalf."

"I shall be happy to tell him everything. I've not said anything so far because you are on holiday and I thought he wouldn't want to talk shop."

She smiled and bade them goodnight.

8

Next morning, Masters and Green left the hotel dining room shortly after half past eight, at which time the Mollers were still eating breakfast.

"Do you want the sergeants with us, George?"

"I've told them to stand by. I'll ask Celia if she minds a big audience. If she agrees to the four of us being present, we'll call them in."

"Fair enough." Green sat down and lit a cigarette. "If four of us talk round this table we can do it quietly. Six of us would be rather a conspicuous crowd at this time in the morning."

"What do you suggest, Bill?"

"The garden. They've got all sorts of seats and tables out there, with sun umbrellas. I can see it all out of my room window. There's another of those big cedars out there. From the looks of it I'd say that the Cardinal's park stretched this far in the old days, until bits were pinched for building on."

"You could well be right. I think he founded the school here, and that stretches down the side of the road that runs past here and then jinks to fringe the arboretum. Ah! Here they are." They rose to their feet as Celia and Harry approached. Harry was carrying two largish books which he put down on the coffee table.

"Travelling reference library," he said. "Celia's nearly as bad as you, George. These are two of those she's brought along for light reading."

Five minutes later they were all sitting round a circular table in the garden. The morning sun was already warm and the flowers in the borders added colour to this very pleasant conference room.

"What is it you would like to know, Mr Masters?"

"Two things basically. I have here a list of birds. Mostly ducks, but including black-headed gulls and moorhens." He handed over a copy of the list he had prepared in advance. As Celia glanced at it, he continued. "Firstly, are any of those birds carnivorous, and secondly, do they all make nests? If they do build nests, would they seek out and use scraps of material—clothing material, that is—for lining the nests."

"May I know why these birds in particular, and their location? Where they are to be found could be important as locations do affect habits."

"That is the list of birds the Christchurch Park authorities say inhabit the lake and the island where we have just found the skeleton of a man."

"The skeleton is on the island?"

"Completely hidden by long grass, bushes and trees. The island is left to naturalize and is tidied up a bit just once a year, in autumn."

Celia nodded. "So the body was put there, fully clothed, presumably after the clearance last autumn, and now it is a totally unclothed skeleton? Is that it?"

"Precisely."

"You wish to know then, whether the birds could have helped to pick the bones clean and to take the clothing?"

"Yes."

Harry Moller said: "George, in a place like that there must be rats, or at least voles, besides other smaller fauna that would take the flesh."

"That had occurred to us, of course. But the clothing? And the other thing is, Harry, that I think the whole operation has been pretty quick. The man disappeared six or seven months ago. I think my two sergeants will tell you that the skeleton looks as though it had been lying there in its present state for several months now, whitening and drying out."

"I see. Perhaps if Celia tells you what she thinks it

will help you to decide the combination of factors."

"Mallard first, because he's a fairly common sort of chap, and so there are probably more of him than the others." She consulted an illustrated book. "As I thought." She looked up. "You can take it that all these birds build nests. What they use for them is a different matter." She again looked at the book. "Mallard usually nest close to the ground but sometimes they use a hollow tree or the abandoned nest of another bird."

"In the air?" asked Tip, in surprise.

"Yes. Particularly if the tree overhangs water. Then the ducklings either fall or are pushed out of the nest and land in the water, if you'll forgive that expression."

"I see."

"Now here's something interesting. They build the nests with leaves or grass and line it with down." She looked across at Masters. "If you were to read scraps of soft material for down. . . ?"

"Would that be likely?"

"I don't see why not if there is a good supply handy. Particularly as they lay their eggs between February and May, a time when soft vegetable material may not be too plentiful. And I suspect that by that time, several months after the body had been deposited, the clothing would be rotting, so that it could be pulled apart quite easily. Their beaks are quite strong, you know."

Masters nodded his acceptance of this opinion. Celia again turned to the book. "Now, as to food." She looked up again. "This is why I asked you where these birds are located. Those that live in places like ponds in parks where people can go and feed them acquire different habits from those that spend their time out in marshes and beside wilder stretches of water. Whereas the strictly natural food of the Mallard, for instance, is mainly seeds, buds and stems of water plants, those that have sausage rolls thrown to them by the public eat what they're given."

"Bully sandwiches?" asked Green.

"As long as there's mustard in them, yes."

191

Green stared at Celia until she smiled. "I think you can definitely say they take some animal food, at least. Because here . . ." She touched the open page with a finger, ". . . it says that some Mallard that live in towns are known to drown sparrows and then swallow them." She looked at Masters. "Ipswich fills the bill—if you will again pardon the expression."

"With pleasure. In fact I can see that Bill Green thoroughly appreciates your sense of humour."

"That's nice. Now for the Moorhen." She turned a few pages. "Their nesting-sites are by the side of ponds or rivers and they feed in marshes or meadows. They build near water, but sometimes some distance away in trees or bushes. There is no mention of them using anything but dried water plants for nests. But this is interesting for you. Their diet appears to be wild fruit, seeds and so on, but also worms, slugs, snails, insects, sometimes the eggs and chicks of other birds and it has been known for a Moorhen to seize and try to drown a homing pigeon by holding it under water."

"To eat it when dead?"

"Presumably."

The conference went on.

Black-headed gulls eat scraps and offal in towns, Celia read; crabs, sand eels, moths, snails and various worms and insects in the wild. Pochards eat small water animals as well as vegetation, and line their nests with soft material, as well as feeding on water plants and water animals, including insects, frogs, spawn and small fish.

At last she closed her books.

"It appears that they are all omnivorous, and that most of them like a soft lining to their nests. Have I answered your questions, Mr Masters?"

"Very fully, thank you, Mrs Moller."

"Here, I say, come on, you two," exclaimed Moller. "This formality! Mr and Mrs indeed!"

"We're doing business," replied his wife. "Now, if George would like to order me coffee, I shall be very happy to have it with him, informally." She smiled at her husband. "But not so informally that you others can't be present and join in. I've done most of the talking so far. I shall sit and listen to you others."

Masters ordered the tray to be brought out to them, and Green was soon regaling Celia with a story about a grumpy neighbour of his when he was a boy. The neighbour in question had been dubbed 'Ticky Whiskers' by Green senior. It appeared that Celia, too, had a similar type of neighbour in her youth. Her father had dubbed this one 'Nitty Tash.'

"Miserly little man. Mean," grunted Green.

"Penny pinching," said Celia. "Let my father have a cupful of cement powder in an old golden-syrup tin to do a little filling in on the garden path. He charged sixpence for the cement and a penny for the tin."

"This could go on all day, Chief," whispered Berger. "When the DCI meets somebody who can cap everything he says. . . ."

"Not to worry," replied Masters. "We've really nothing much to do today."

Half an hour later the Mollers left to visit the bird observatory at Walberswick and the areas round Benacre. As soon as they were gone, Green said, "Having a conversation with that lass is like talking to myself. I know all the replies and answers before they come."

"Except when it comes to birds," suggested Berger.

"There's that," admitted Green. "Bully sandwiches as long as they've got mustard in them, indeed!"

"You asked for it."

"Perhaps I did." He looked across at Masters. "Day off, today, is it?"

"Almost. We'll meet briefly this evening at six in my room. Apart from that, just two things."

"Such as?"

"You two," he said to Tip and Berger, "are not known at The Capercaillie. You will visit today—I suggest at tea time—and discover for me what sort of cakes they sell. You don't have to eat any you don't want to, but please note the full selection on offer. Also, discover who decorates them. Select a seat so that you can, if necessary, see right through the office into the kitchen. Understood?"

"Got it, Chief."

"Remember, you are not police officers."

"Courting couple," said Green. "Hold hands across the table an' all that. Wonderful what questions you can ask and get answers to when people see you are in that state. They fall over themselves to show that all the world loves a lover."

"We've acted the part before," said Tip simply.

Green was about to ask her a question, but stopped. Instead he turned to Masters. "You said two things, George."

"Yes. You and I will recce the route we think the body took."

"From Kempe's house to the island?"

"Yes. I'd like to make sure it is not only possible, but absolutely probable."

"Get you. Make sure there's no electric fence in between. That sort of thing."

"Terrain mostly, I think. But, yes. Make sure there's no great impediment."

"There'll be no sign after all this time."

"That would be too much to hope for. So, by now, Berger, you and Tip can have the car for the day if you want it. You can drop the DCI and myself fairly close to Kempe's place and we will walk down to the park gates. We'll get a cab back or, if necessary, drop in on DCI Knight to cadge a lift."

"Sure you wouldn't like a run to the sea, Chief?" asked Berger. "Gin and tonic overlooking the briny, with fish and chips to follow. There's Felixstowe within spitting distance."

Masters shook his head. "I want to be handy in case the pathologist sparks."

"In that case," said Tip, "I'll change into a most unpolicelike sundress and you," she said to Berger, "can get

194

into an open-neck shirt and find a plastic bag for carrying the sticks of rock home in."

By a quarter past eleven Masters and Green had been dropped between the Kempe house and the park entrance it was assumed they had used.

They walked slowly along the narrow way which was almost a replica of the one they had used near The Blenheim.

"Easy," said Green. "Berger tells me those little Honda vans carry a thousand pounds. Call it eight hundredweight. They're pretty small. One could come down here at night and be out of sight if pulled in close under one wall, on the shady side. These trees overhang so far you could camouflage a squadron of tanks down here."

"Lovers' lane?" queried Masters.

"In summer, perhaps. Not in November. It's too windy in this neck of the woods in winter for any couple to want to hang about outside for body-clutching purposes. My guess is they'd have it all to themselves."

"Here's the gate."

"They're mighty inconsistent," growled Green. "They've got gates fourteen feet high down in the town, but up on our side and here they're no more than four feet."

"Easy enough to tumble a body over and follow it yourself, particularly working from the height of the back of a van. Or side, rather. Those vans have sliding doors at the sides, so I imagine they pulled in close rather than backed in."

They entered the park. For two or three yards the surface was level, and then they were on the crest, looking down at the whole panorama of the park. The ground, falling away at their feet, was smooth grass.

"No false crests as far as I can see," said Green, "and you can just see the lake through that little clump of trees down there."

"False crests?" asked Masters.

"Hidden dips," explained Green. "They'd make pulling a body pretty difficult."

"There's just one thing, Bill. The path that leads across from this gate seems to go round the north of the hill, but I think it joins the main one from the gate near The Blenheim. If they had some sort of barrow or trolley. . . ."

"Downhill all the way," agreed Green. "The weight of the body would take itself down."

They descended gently, looking about them as they went. Green was particularly keen, stopping every so often to look back to make sure they were keeping more or less in a straight line. "Nothing so far to prevent a very easy haul," he said. "Not many people about up here, so it's a pity we didn't get young Berger to put Tip on a blanket and try it out. We could have estimated the time it would have taken."

"Better still," said Masters, "we could try it this evening after the gates are closed. Knight could arrange for us to be let out. We'd get ourselves in by the method we think the Kempes used."

"Good idea," said Green. "Well, here we are. Flattening out now for the last twenty yards."

They walked in silence to the rails and stood looking at the ducks and the island. Green said, after a minute or two, "Hello, here's our old mate, the keeper, doing his rounds."

As the keeper came abreast, Masters gave him good morning. Recognizing them, he stopped and accepted the cigarette Green offered him.

"Do you get much litter?" asked Masters, innocently. "Most people seem to use the bins provided, but I expect some ignore them."

"Funny thing, bor," said the keeper. "Even the kids don't drop stuff about. I think some of the adults would tell 'em if they did. No, our trouble is old ladies, mostly."

"Old ladies dropping litter?"

"No. pinching slippings mostly, though I have known them take whole plants. Mostly they come in here with a pair of secateurs hidden in a bag, and when they think nobody's looking they whip a bit off anything they fancy.

196

Then when they get it home they turn it into cuttings. Just after the bushes have flowered is the worst time. Soft wood cuttings, you know, bor, slipped into a pot of peat and coarse sand. Nice old things, they are, too, when they're not out wi' their secateurs."

"There's no telling what people will do," said Masters, trying to sound suitably amazed. "With us it's supermarket trolleys. They park in a side road, best part of half a mile from the shop. Then they push their goods to where they've parked, load the stuff in the boot and drive off leaving the trolley. I've seen as many as half a dozen at a time left like that. But then, I don't suppose you get supermarket trolleys as there's no parking in here."

"No," replied the keeper. "We don't have trouble with trolleys. No, I tell a lie. We don't have trouble as a reg'lar thing, but I can remember, not all that long ago . . . when would it be? . . . last winter some time . . . there was one. Just about here where we're standing now. Funny thing that. Two of us walked this way together when we were closing up an' it weren't here then. Stands to reason two of us wouldn't miss it on a path this wide, an' that's what I said in the office when they said we'd overlooked it. Didn't overlook it next morning either, bor. Here it was, large as life an' twice as nasty."

"Kids?" asked Green.

"Course it was kids. Up to some little game. The big 'uns can climb out in places, you know, so they'll hide— not often, like—but now an' again, when we turn everybody out. Little devils. They'd a' brought that trolley in and hidden it, an' afterwards played games with it. Riding along the paths an' the like. I know that's what they done because that trolley wasn't like it should a' been. Not that they're very good at the best o' times, but this one was really down on its axles. Our lass in the office rang the shop to tell 'em to come an' collect it an' the ole bor who came was pretty disgusted about it. Cost twenty quid, 'e said, an' them young lads riding around in it had just about finished it for good, 'e said. Almost blamed us for letting 'em do it, 'e did, so I told him to charge a five quid deposit then they wouldn't be pinched."

Masters smiled as the park keeper stubbed the cigarette on the instep of his boot and then palmed the dog-end to drop in the nearest litter bin.

"Well, bor, I'd best be off."

"Cherrio, mate," said Green. "Be seeing you."

"Do you feel like a pub lunch in town, Bill?" asked Masters, "or shall we get a car back to The Blenheim?"

"Pub lunch will do me," said Green. "Ploughman's. Then we'll still be close by to drop in on Harold Knight afterwards."

"I was going to ring you, Mr Masters. The pathologist has been on."

"Interim report?"

"Sort of. He said he was going to tell the coroner that he'd got a complete skeleton there. No breaks, no bullet holes or anything of that kind. And none of the organs or flesh, either. Evidently larvae and insects have cleaned the skull out completely, so there's no brain tissue he can test either. So the cause of death for the coroner will not be specific, with the possibility of poisoning being only one of the options, along with natural causes, exposure and all the rest of them. And because he can't specify which poison, if any, could be implicated, the pathologist has asked the coroner to decide whether he would be justified in going on with very lengthy and expensive tests to try and identify a possibly non-existent poison. Evidently the pathologist thinks the man would have died so soon after ingesting the poison that there wouldn't have been time for any toxic substance to get into the bones. What do you think?"

"Unfortunately, I think the pathologist is right."

"Well, it's up to the coroner now, but what will you do?"

"Press on," said Masters. "We're so nearly home we

must try to get there by another route. And by the way, there is something you could do for us, if you would."

"Say the word."

Masters recounted the story of how he and Green had set out to show how the body had got to the lake, and how the park-keeper had found the supermarket trolley near the vital spot. "Could you check up on that for us, please?"

"I'll have to go to the park office to find out which supermarket it was, so the girl who did the phoning may remember the date. Then the shop may have a record of its recovery. I doubt it, in both cases, but I can try. Shall I also try to discover if the Kempes shop there?"

"By all means, but it need not necessarily be relevant. Anybody can pick up one of those trolleys at any car park, these days."

Knight nodded. "They're everywhere," he agreed.

Masters thanked Knight and got to his feet.

"Any chance of a lift up to The Blenheim, Harold? We walked down, but it's a bit hot to trek up again, and I'd like to call in at the hospital on the way."

"Your wagon in dock, is it?"

"His Nibs here gave the kids a small job to do, so they've got the car," grunted Green.

"In that case. . . ." Knight picked up a phone and ordered a beat car to call in for Masters and Green.

At the early evening conference in his room, Masters and his team ran through the whole case including the pathologist's interim and, depending on the coroner, possibly final, report.

"What do we do, Chief?" asked Berger. "Attend the inquest and press for an exhaustive examination of the skeleton?"

Masters shook his head. "The DCI and I think we still could have one shot left in the locker. You will remember that from the outset we have been using what, for a better term, we have called the spot-the-difference technique. This afternoon, on our way back from the police station, we called in at the hospital. Our aim was to consult the pharmacist."

"For poisons information, Chief?"

"Not exactly. You are probably not aware of this, but each year there is published a book called Data Sheet Compendium. It has an alphabetical index of every prescribable drug and medicine in the country, together with the names of the manufacturers and all the information concerning each particular drug that a doctor need know before prescribing it, and which the government insists should be made public.

"Playing spot the difference, we called on the pharmacist at the hospital as the most likely person to have copies of this Compendium on his shelves. We asked if we could consult the present one to see what products AVL is making at the moment and to compare this list with the one for five years ago when the Kempes last worked for AVL."

"Why exactly, Chief?" asked Tip.

"Because, over the last few years, the statutory provisions concerning the sale and supply of medicines have changed considerably. For instance, the barbiturates were widely used a few years ago, but now they are frowned on and consequently rarely prescribed. The result is that drug makers, or some of them, no longer produce medicines containing barbiturates."

Berger and Tip still seemed bewildered.

"Mr Green and I thought that if we could compare the two lists we should see whether AVL had stopped production of any of the products they made five years ago. If there were any such drugs there could just be the possibility that among those that had been stopped was one in what we might call the dangerous category—speaking purely from our point of view."

"I don't follow this, Chief," complained Tip. "If Packard was poisoned six or seven months ago, it would have been with a substance that is still available, and not with one that was stopped years ago."

"Wrong, love," said Green, shaking his head. "Don't you remember Mrs Packard saying that her husband still had old samples from his AVL days in the spare bedroom? The Kempes were reps for AVL at the same time, remember. They'd have exactly the same samples for handing out. So why shouldn't they still have a few left, as Packard did?"

"But I was told in training that reps can't hand out drugs just like that. Doctors have to ask for them in writing and the drug companies have to keep very strict accounts of what is handed out."

"They do, love, these days. But there's something else to remember. There's a difference between pills, capsules and bottles of jallop that patients put in their mouths and something they get to rub on their skins to relieve sprains and strains. As much difference as there is between a tin of orange juice and a tin of petrol. You can drink one very safely, you can't the other."

"And AVL make a lot of ointments and . . . what is the word? . . . topical medicines?"

"That's right," said Masters. "Topical meaning for external use only, or rather for local use, which in this case amounts to the same thing."

"And topical medicines or rubs or whatever can contain substances that would kill you if taken internally?"

"Right. When I used to play sport, everybody used to use what was known as White Liniment for strained muscles, sprains and, indeed, as a general massage medium. Every chemist in those days made it up and bottled it for himself. As I remember, the principal ingredients were eggs and turpentine with some sort of dilute acid and ammonia."

"I remember the stuff, Chief," said Berger. "It's still used in police gyms."

"Is it, indeed!"

"Yes Chief. Pongs of turpentine. Not a bad smell, actually."

"Quite. My point is that though turpentine is used in very small amounts in just one or two internal prepara-

201

tions like Dutch Drops and also—by a different route—for enemas, it is a toxic substance, so much so that three small teaspoonfuls full of the stuff have been fatal in children. And yet it is widely bought in White Liniment without prescription."

"But nobody would drink the stuff, Chief."

"Agreed. As you say, it pongs, and smell being a large factor in taste, nobody would willingly drink it. But what if the ingredients of some such preparation did not smell at all? I agree that people who knew what it was would not drink it. But what if it were fed to some unknowing person? Forced upon him, not perhaps by might and main, but by an equally potent agency—the belief that he is among those who will do him no harm. . . ."

"Like friends and acquaintances, Chief?"

"Yes. Among such people, so that he is off guard to the extent that he will not question what he may be given to eat or drink or even suppose that it may be poisonous."

"I like that way of putting it," said Green. "That one's own beliefs can be as strong a force as muscle in another person." He looked across at Masters. "You can carry on now, George. Don't mind me."

"Thanks," said Masters, drily, before turning back to the sergeants. "I gave you two a job to do today. What happened?"

Berger said: "We got the information, Chief. Several people decorate the cakes. Apparently the demand is so great for outside as well as inside catering that on most days one person couldn't cope. Mrs Kempe is usually one of those who does the cakes because her ordinary chefs have the afternoons off."

"That figures," said Green. "They've to come on again at night for dinners."

"That's it. So Mrs Kempe usually supervises cakes with a middle-aged woman who's a part-timer, unless they're really pushed, and one of the waitresses to help her. There's cream to be put in cakes and fancies and pastries. . . ."

"They've got real cream-horns and brandy snaps with

cream in," said Tip, enthusiastically. "But the waitress told me they couldn't call them brandy-snaps any more because of EEC regulations. Ginger snaps now. Not nearly so nice a name."

"In that case," asked Green, "why can they still call them cream-horns? The damn things aren't made of horn. The trouble with the Common Market is it's common. And if I weren't a gent I'd say common as muck."

After a pause, Berger went on. "And we could see them through the office walls scattering icing sugar and those little coloured things, as well as using sheets of chocolate squares. They looked like big postage stamps."

"And sheets and sheets of little violets and pink and white roses. . . ."

"Don't go on, petal," groaned Green. "You're beginning to make me feel I missed something."

"Oh, we didn't have any of them. We just saw most of it going on. That woman has a mirror in her office, like they have in shops, and we could see. . . ."

"How very convenient," said Masters. "You saw Mrs Kempe at work?"

"Yes, Chief," replied Berger. "She was on the cream cakes today. She'd got a lot of little sponge buns, scooping the tops out. She filled the hole with cream and then cut the lid in two, sticking the halves back at an angle above the cream."

"Fairy cakes, Chief," said Tip. "She finished them off with a dusting of icing sugar."

"Thank you. No more about cakes, please. You've told me what I wanted to know and it is of great value."

"You mean Mrs Kempe gave Packard something in a cream cake, Chief?"

"Why not, Tip? We know he doted on sweet, creamy cakes, don't we? A place like The Capercaillie was bound to come to his attention sooner or later. There is every chance he went in there at four o'clock one day and ordered himself a pot of tea and a plate of cream cakes."

"You mean Mrs Kempe saw him and immediately doctored his cakes, Chief?" asked Berger.

"She can see everybody in the restaurant from her office, can't she? And she wouldn't have forgotten about Packard's obsession with cakes. She wouldn't have forgotten anything about him."

"In fact," said Green, "it's on the cards that remembering the way he ate gooey cakes she was expecting him to arrive sooner or later and had prepared for his coming."

"By having something ready to put in the cakes? Something tasteless?" asked Tip.

Green nodded. "That's just what His Nibs has been explaining to you. Packard went into The Capercaillie in the belief that what he was given to eat and drink would be wholesome. So he scoffed it. But it wasn't wholesome. It killed him. Not on the spot, of course, otherwise we'd have heard about it. But a bit later, away from the restaurant."

Berger turned to Masters. "Did you discover in the old Compendium a product that could be poisonous and tasteless and which AVL don't make nowadays?"

"Yes."

"What was it, Chief?" asked Tip.

"A powder for baby's bottoms."

There was a long silence while the sergeants stared in disbelief.

"True enough," said Green at last. "Somebody had the bright idea of calling it Be Te Em powder."

"BTM?"

"More or less."

"The old Victorian way of referring to . . . to the rear end?" asked Tip.

"Not so much of your Victorian," retorted Green. "The expression was still in wide use in my young days."

"Same thing," grinned Berger.

"Watch it," growled Green. "The penalty for impertinence is very costly. A double gin at least."

"Talking of which," said Masters, "shall we push on?" He looked at Tip. "Have you ever heard of Hexachlorophane?"

She shook her head.

"No, Chief."

"According to my medical dictionary it is an antiseptic which is active against a wide range of micro-organisms, and it retains its activity in the presence of soap. So it is often used in soaps and creams in a concentration of one to two per cent, but it must be used with caution in babies as it can be absorbed through the skin and prove harmful. But please remember, that is the gist of what is written in an up-to-date dictionary.

"Another book I have on toxic substances and their effects, published in 1974, makes no mention of Hexachlorophane."

"Spot the difference," murmured Berger.

"Quite. The real authority, however, has lots to say. First off, it says that Hexachlorophane is a white, tasteless powder, insoluble in water."

"Meaning," said Berger, "that it could be whipped into stiff cream and not be seen or tasted and bingo!"

"You're jumping the gun a bit, Sergeant, but yes. That is the case in a nutshell. If Hexachlorophane is taken by mouth—in quite weak concentrations—it can cause death. But before that, any or all of the following effects could be felt. Nausea, vomiting, diarrhoea, abdominal pain, dehydration, shock, convulsions and coma. Several cases are mentioned where adults have died after ingestion and where babies have suffered brain damage from the use of Hexachlorophane dusting powders, soaps and skin cleansing liquids. Indeed, it is thought that a wrongly manufactured baby powder—in France—caused the deaths of more than twenty babies. A manufacturing error caused the powder to be sent out with six per cent Hexachlorophane instead of a much smaller amount. And when I say smaller, I mean smaller. In many countries, preparations containing more than three-quarters of one per cent of Hexachlorophane are not available except on medical prescription.

"But to cut a long story short, about six mils of Hexachlorophane proper would kill an adult. That is a fairly big teaspoonful. At the time Kempe was a rep, AVL were selling Be Te Em dusting powder with three per cent Hexachlorophane in it. Now they produce nothing containing Hexachlorophane. It was used for nappy rash and such like skin infections and presumably, as with all their other similar products, reps carried sample supplies to give away quite freely to doctors."

"Chief!" Tip put one hand to her mouth. "That box we saw Annabel Kempe bring from the house. . . ."

"Yes, Tip. We shall probably never know, but I think it was a box of Be Te Em samples. My belief is that, expecting Packard to call in at her restaurant at some unspecified time in the future, Mrs Kempe took several of those samples to The Capercaillie to be in readiness should her expectations prove to be right. What I think you saw was Mrs Kempe getting rid of her remaining stock of the powder."

"But, Chief," objected Berger. "When Mrs Kempe was a rep, Hexachlorophane wasn't known to be so lethal as it now is. How would she know the powder would kill Packard?"

"That's easy," said Green. "Annabel Kempe was expecting a baby. I reckon she was stocking up with this Be Te Em powder to use on the child when it came. And on others that might follow. Also, she was a rep, knew about medicines, and being interested in the subject, would read everything about them that came her way. And she still had pals in AVL who would tell her that the powder was being withdrawn and why. So she wouldn't be unaware of its toxicity. In fact, once she heard it was a dicey substance, she could make it her business to learn all about it. All these reference books are in libraries, you know."

"And when she got to know, she determined to keep it to kill off Packard? That's farfetched."

"Is it, love? I could give you quite a good argument saying not only did she keep that powder for knocking off Packard, but also that she opened that restaurant and made it what it is in the sure and certain knowledge that by doing so she would lure him into her trap. Think about it. How many restaurants of that calibre do you know that serve tea like a café behind a confectioner's shop. Open morning, noon, teatime and night was her motto, just to be sure she attracted Packard. And the name of the restaurant? The Capercaillie. The big grouse! Do you think that name came by chance? She'd got a big grouse—with a fat snipe—and she intended to ease it. Nowhere do they mention the name Kempe on their fascia board or on their van. Why? Perhaps it was because they hoped that just one man wouldn't get to know who owned it before his greed had taken him inside its doors to get what was coming to him."

"Is all this true, Chief?" asked Tip.

"What I think the DCI was doing was putting up an argument that prosecuting council might use at a trial."

"It sounded very convincing."

"Possibly because it has the ring of truth, or at least elements of truth. You were the one who said that long-term preparations for murdering Packard on the part of Mrs Kempe were far fetched. The DCI and I don't agree with you."

"Sorry, Chief."

"Don't be sorry. Say what you think. But, please think before you say at moments like this."

Tip reddened. "I did think, Chief. It's just that I didn't think in the same way as you and Mr Green."

Masters smiled. "Then you left something out of your calculations. It's easily done." He generalized the conversation. "That is how matters stand at the moment. We think we know how, and we think we know why, and we think we know where. We even think we know how the body was transported from the Kempe house to the island. But that leaves a gap. If Packard was poisoned in the restaurant, what happened to him between the time he ate the cream cakes and his last journey to the island?"

Tip said: "Chief, Mr Green says the Kempes have been plotting this murder for some time. Years, maybe."

"Please go on."

"It would be right to suppose then that they had made provision for what they did. What I mean is, they wouldn't let Packard escape from The Capercaillie to pass out later in the street where he could be picked up and rushed to hospital for his life to be saved."

"Good point," growled Green.

Tip reddened. "I know that if I owned The Capercaillie, I wouldn't only have a private office there. A woman who works the long hours Mrs Kempe does needs somewhere to rest and freshen. She's got to appear in mint condition at all times if you know what I mean. So I think that somewhere on the premises will be a sitting room and bathroom—private suite, if you like—for the exclusive use of the Kempes. After he had eaten his cream cakes, couldn't he have been invited to have a drink or a chat or, if he was already feeling groggy, a lie down in the private room? Until he passed out altogether and then . . . well, he could have been taken in the van, not to the Kempe house, but direct to the park entrance which they knew and had selected in advance."

"Excellent," said Masters. "You and Sergeant Berger, still using your courting couple disguise if you like, had better set out to test your theory."

"Tonight, Chief?" asked Berger.

"Whenever you like. But there is going to be an answer one way or another. Whichever it is, I'd like it by tomorrow at this time."

"It should be easy, Chief," replied Tip. "All Sergeant Berger has to do is to sweetheart it out of the little waitress who fell for him this afternoon. My guess is that she thought she might stand a chance of stealing him from me if she played her cards right. And I daresay she might think the right cards to play will be to answer any question he might ask her."

"You're only jealous," laughed Berger.

"Why should I be jealous?" asked Tip, stiffly.

"Right," said Masters, exchanging glances with Green. "Time for a little smackerel of something, I think."

Harry Moller and Celia were in the bar when the four of them walked in.

"How did the day go?" asked Celia as they all congregated at the far end of the bar where it widened out beyond the counter.

"Fairly well-ish," grinned Masters. "But like every other day, it brought its problems. How were the birds?"

"Ornithologically interesting." She smiled.

"Don't use words like that," protested Green. "Not before I have a potable concoction of spiritous liquor in my hand."

Celia laughed. "Naturally, Harry can't tell me much about his work. It being of a secret nature, as they say. But he has mentioned your team from time to time. It seems to me he gets more kick out of working with your lot than most of the others he has to deal with."

"Your lot?" queried Green with a grimace.

"Sorry. Ah! here's your drink. Cheers."

She and Green continued their badinage and were joined by the two sergeants. It gave Masters the opportunity he wanted to take Moller aside.

"Hexachlorophane, you say, George?"

"I'm pretty sure of it, but it's going to be very difficult to prove, if we ever manage it."

Moller thought for a moment or two, then he asked: "Are there any rats on the island? I know we've talked of voles. They are rat-like and are called water-rats of course, but I'm referring to the genuine article. The authentic *genus mus*."

"I don't know."

"Find out. And if there are, trap some."

"Just like that?"

"Yes. Get a keeper or the corporation rodent operative or whatever his name is these days to look for and trap them."

"Dead?"

"Or alive. It doesn't matter. But get them you must if you want to prove your point."

209

"And then?"

"Deliver them to the local forensic laboratory and ask Chief Inspector Knight to arrange for me to use their facilities for a couple of hours. That shouldn't be too hard to fix. I'm in the government service, after all."

"And that's it?"

"That's it."

"What about your holiday?"

"Celia's going off tomorrow to see some friends of hers in the bird world who live up the coast."

"Would you care to tell me what you are proposing?"

"I don't want to raise your hopes too high, George."

"Fair enough. I think I can guess something of what you intend to do."

"I expect you can. Shall we leave it at that and join in the fun? Bill Green and my missus seem to be amusing themselves and the others."

"They appear to be on somewhat similar wavelengths, Celia and Bill."

"What the Scots call pawky, I believe."

"That sounds about right."

The next day, Masters felt matters were out of his hands. After getting permission for Moller to use the police laboratories and persuading the local authority to set baited rat traps on the island, there was little he and Green could usefully do. He had kept the car for his own use, knowing that Berger and Tip could easily walk down into the town to make their clandestine enquiries at The Capercaillie.

It was Green who said: "There are some paperbacks stacked on the desk in the foyer. Choose one, and we'll go and sit in the park. Not near the island. Up this end, on my bench, near the giant cedar."

By half past eleven they were installed, pleasantly shaded from the heat of the sun, but faced with a glorious prospect and close enough to passers by to look up and say good morning to those who returned their gaze.

"One thing, Bill," said Masters after some minutes.

"You said to Tip yesterday that a Capercaillie was a big grouse. How did you know that?"

"I didn't, not really. It just sort of came out. But the funny thing is that I was right."

"You checked up with Celia Moller, presumably."

"Yes. It is a sort of grouse, or at least it has many of the same characteristics. And it is big. She told me the cock capercaillie is much the largest bird to be seen in our fir forests. She said they could be mistaken for flying turkeys as some of them weigh about seventeen pounds."

"I don't think I've ever seen one."

"There aren't any down here. Only in Scotland. But I don't think I would like to meet one, unsuspectingly, that is."

"Why not?"

"Young Celia said that the cock birds defend their territories so fiercely that they attack dogs and human beings as well as other birds that stray inside their boundaries."

"There's a moral there, somewhere," said Masters.

Green grunted and closed his eyes sleepily. Masters left him to snooze.

It was in the bar at The Blenheim, just before one o'clock that Berger and Tip presented themselves.

"From the looks on your faces," said Green, "you've struck oil."

"That's right. There is a private sitting room. Where do you think it is?"

"Above the shop."

"No, below it. In the cellar. Down there is the wine store too."

"Naturally. And it is always kept locked and only the Kempes have keys."

"That's about it, but various people have to go down there to get wines that are asked for and are not in the ready-use racks upstairs. But the thing is this sitting room, or changing room, that the Kempes have set up down there is also usually kept locked, because the safe is in there. Cleaners go in, of course, but Mrs Kempe

211

keeps it all strictly private. There's a loo and handbasin, as well. Our information is that it is very pretty and nicely furnished. Actually, Chief, I thought you'd like to know that it is actually only a semi-basement. There is a window, half below ground. I examined it pretty closely. There are lined velvet curtains on the inside."

"I expect there are. There would be no privacy otherwise, because one has to use a light at any time in most places like that."

"That's it, Chief."

"Did you discover whether, apart from members of staff, the Kempes ever invite anybody else down there?"

"Sorry, Chief. There didn't seem any way I could wangle out that bit of information."

"Never mind. You've done very well."

That afternoon they all went to the park. Tip and Berger lay on the grass to soak up the sun. Green snoozed, and Masters went through his case, mentally, occasionally making notes in his pocket book. It was after four o'clock when Harry Moller came striding up the path, obviously making for The Blenheim. Masters rose quietly and went towards him.

"Hello, George. I didn't know you were here."

"I've got the three sleepers with me."

"No you haven't," said Green, who had apparently overheard the conversation from a distance of some yards. "Come and sit down, you two. You're making the place look untidy."

They joined him on the seat.

"Well, Harry?"

"You were right, George. He was poisoned with Hexachlorophane."

"Now how in heaven's name have you been able to prove that?" demanded Green.

"We'd all like to hear," said Berger, sitting up and prodding Tip into wakefulness.

"Quite easily, really," said Moller, "once we had some rats which had been caught on the island. You know that animal tests are carried out on all substances which

212

are going to be used in or on humans. In the case of Hexachlorophane there were studies in rats and monkeys. I guessed at rats, actually, because they are the most commonly used subjects, and I assumed there were no monkeys on your island. So, I reckoned that if some of any colony of rats there might be could be trapped, I could get to work.

"It sounds ghastly, I know, but you have to face the fact that the flesh of Packard's body was eaten by animals and insects, and the most voracious of these was likely to be the rat.

"If Packard had ingested a large amount of Hexachlorophane it would, by the time he died, have invaded large parts of his body, particularly the organs. It follows then that any animal that ate any of his body would also be ingesting Hexachlorophane. I need hardly remind you that a minute amount of any such substance would constitute a very large dose for a rat and so those that stayed at the table until it was bare could well have built up a concentration that would have some effect upon them.

"I therefore went to the forensic lab and read up on the synopses of trials with Hexachlorophane in animals, knowing that if I could find the same toxic effects that were shown in the trials to be affecting any of the rats that were caught, I would have positive proof that they had been exposed to a source of the drug which could only have been Packard's body. If I didn't find the toxic effects, however, it would not mean that you were wrong. Merely that I couldn't produce proof for you."

"I needed fairly mature rats. Well over six or seven months old, for obvious reasons."

"They had to be old enough to have fed off the corpse," said Green.

"Quite. Well, I won't go into technical details, but rats which were fed Hexachlorophane developed weakness of the hindquarters after two weeks, and this later progressed to paralysis. Three or four months later, when some of the rats were autopsied—please note, they were still living until that time—cystic vesiculation was present in the white matter of the brain. And before you ask, that means the formation of little bladders or sacs or blisters, if you like, and I don't know what, if anything, they contained.

"Today, quite simply, among quite a large number of rats presented to me very quickly by an able young rat catcher I found both hindquarter weakness and cystic vesiculation of the brain in mature rats. I had to sacrifice three of them. The others are being taken back to the island to be caught again should you need them to be, George. But we have the necessary affidavits for you. Sworn and signed that the rats I tested came from the island and were not fed after capture and so on and so on." He shrugged. "You cracked it, chums."

"Thanks, Harry," said Masters. "Your help has been invaluable."

"Pleased to be in on it, but you should know that had you told the local forensic people that you suspected Hexachlorophane they would have done the same for you."

"I'm sure they would have done, but Bill and I only began to suspect Hexachlorophane late yesterday afternoon, shortly before I spoke to you."

"Good. Now I'm going to The Blenheim for one of their excellent cream teas. Anybody care to join me?"

There were no takers.

"I tell you what," said Green. "Let's walk down and tip it all in Harold Knight's lap. Then we can have a party this evening and go home tomorrow morning."

"Fetch the car, Tip," said Masters. "Meet us at the main gate. We'll do as the DCI suggests. Then the only chore will be to go home and report the case closed to Mr Anderson."

"I wonder what his Capercaillie will be like when he hears it?" mused Green.

"As he in turn will have to explain to Beryl, I think his grouse will be as big as Mrs Kempe's."

There's an epidemic with 27 million victims. And no visible symptoms.

It's an epidemic of people who can't read.

Believe it or not, 27 million Americans are functionally illiterate, about one adult in five.

The solution to this problem is you... when you join the fight against illiteracy. So call the Coalition for Literacy at toll-free **1-800-228-8813** and volunteer.

**Volunteer
Against Illiteracy.
The only degree you need
is a degree of caring.**

Ad Council Coalition for Literacy